ABOUT THE AUTHOR

When Geoffrey McSkimming was a boy he
found an old motion-picture projector and a tin
containing a dusty film in his grandmother's attic.
He screened the film and was transfixed by
the flickering image of a man in a jaunty pith helmet,
baggy Sahara shorts and special desert sun-spectacles.
The man had an imposing macaw and a clever looking
camel, and Geoffrey McSkimming was mesmerized
by their activities in black-and-white Egypt, Peru,
Greece, and other exotic locations.

Years later he discovered the identities of the trio,
and he has spent much of his time since then retracing
their footsteps, interviewing surviving members of the
Old Relics Society, and gradually reconstructing these
lost true tales which have become the enormously
successful Cairo Jim Chronicles.

To research *Cairo Jim and the Quest for the
Quetzal Queen* Geoffrey McSkimming journeyed
through Mexico, where he visited (and climbed)
all of the ancient pyramids climbed by Cairo Jim,
Doris and Brenda the Wonder Camel.

For Belinda,
who climbed with me to the tops of many
of the Mexican pyramids and temples.

First published in Great Britain 2007 by Walker Books Ltd
87 Vauxhall Walk, London SE11 5HJ

2 4 6 8 10 9 7 5 3 1

Text © 1997 Geoffrey McSkimming
Cover illustration © 2007 Martin Chatterton

The right of Geoffrey McSkimming to be identified as author of
this work has been asserted by him in accordance with the
Copyright, Designs and Patents Act 1988.

This book has been typeset in Plantin

Printed in Great Britain by
Cox & Wyman Ltd, Reading, Berkshire

British Library Cataloguing in Publication Data:
a catalogue record for this book is available from the British Library.

ISBN 978-1-4063-0543-2

www.walkerbooks.co.uk

CAIRO JIM

AND THE QUEST FOR
THE QUETZAL QUEEN

A Mayan Tale of Marvels

GEOFFREY McSKIMMING

WALKER
BOOKS

▲▲▲▲▲ CONTENTS ▲▲▲▲▲

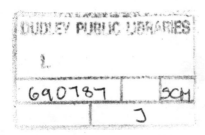

A WORD TO MY READERS

Since the first published Cairo Jim adventure appeared, many letters have poured in from discerning and curious readers eager to find out more clues about Cairo Jim's life. Not to mention the lives of his friends, colleagues and even his arch-enemy, Neptune F. Bone.

Perhaps the most frequently asked question is: *how old is Cairo Jim?*

While I am researching the Cairo Jim Chronicles, I discover many things about the archaeologist-poet and his contemporaries. When I went to Mexico to research this story, and to follow in the man's very footsteps, I discovered something quite overwhelming.

If you read this account, you, too, might find the answer – for yourself – to this most asked-about question.

G. McS.

Part One:

THE KILLING OF TIME?

BACKSTAGE AT THE CAIRO GAIETY THEATRE

"COME ON IN if you're tall, rich and 'andsome!"

Mademoiselle Fifi Glusac, the world's most famous harmonica player and simultaneous contortionist, was in the middle of wiping off her stage make-up after her performance when the insistent knockings on her dressing-room door had burst forth like a series of small, flabby, hiccupping thunderclaps.

The door opened and the figure of a man entered, envapoured in a thick and cheaply aromatic cloud of smoke that was rising from the cigar he held in his pudgy fingers. "Tall?" he said in a deep and pillowy voice. "I think not. Rich? My greatness is yet to be fully recognised. Handsome? My dear mother always described me thus."

Fifi Glusac stared at the figure reflected in her light-bulb-framed dressing-table mirror. She blinked for a few moments at the strangeness of his appearance, then put down her cleansing sponge and turned to face him.

The man raised the cigar to his fleshy lips and took a long suck on it. He exhaled slowly, as though all the world had been waiting for the smoke to escape from his toothpit's inner regions. As it curled out into his

ginger-brown beard, and up through his heavy eyebrows to dissolve above his custard-coloured fez with the Adriatic-blue tassel, his eyes gleamed and his lips smiled.

"Ooh la la," Fifi said, fluffing up her dazzling blonde curls and eyeing him up and down, "and 'oo might you be?"

"I *might* be Orson Welles, the famous film director, but I am not. My name, mademoiselle, is Zoomah. Montgomery Zoomah."

"Pleased to make your acquaintance, M'sieur Zoomah."

"You may call me *Monty*." Without waiting to be asked, he moved further into the dressing room and squeezed all of his substantiality (and there was much of it) into a small armchair. He squirmed until he was comfortable, pulling down his emerald-green waistcoat so that it covered his bulging paunch, and straightening the upper-leg areas of his chequered plus-fours trousers (in order to avoid creasing).

Fifi Glusac tightened her swansdown-trimmed dressing gown more securely around her waist. "And you may call moi *La Stupenda*. Well, what can I do for you, Monty?"

"Ah, no, La Stupenda, it's more of a question of what *I* can do for *you*." He took another puff on the wretched-smelling tobacco and this time blew the smoke out in a firm, somehow *promising*, shaft that shot straight to the chandelier above them.

"Okay zen, what can *you* do for *moi*?"

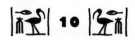

Pausing only to crack his knuckles loudly and to fix her with a glinting eye, he launched himself, like an over-inflated dinghy upon the waves of conversation, into his reason for visiting:

"My dear mademoiselle, I have come to you tonight on a matter of what you might call *artifice*. The whole Realm of Pretending has led me here, you might say. As you well know, the world is full of it, this pretending. Why, in your profession, it is how you make your living, is it not?"

Fifi Glusac stood and put her hands on her feather-lined hips. "Say, what are you insinuating? Zat I don't blow all zose tunes myself? Listen, m'sieur, I know it looks impossible, shoving my feet back behind my 'ead and playing 'Ze Flight of ze Bumble-Bee' on ze 'armonica while I wriggle my toes in perfect rhythm, but I can assure you it's real! I ain't no Mime Artiste. Every contortion I turn, every note I play, is *ALL MY OWN WORK!*"

The man raised his hands in front of himself. "My dear Mademoiselle Glusac—"

"La Stupenda!"

"My dear La Stupenda, I assure you I meant to cast no assertions that you are not genuine in your talents."

"Everyone's a critic, for goodness' sake. You try bending over backwards to earn your living, and see 'ow easy it is!"

"I was merely implying that the profession of the theatre is built on a pretence, is it not? All entertainers are doing some sort of pretending when they are performing, wouldn't you agree?"

She sniffed and sat down again. "I guess so," she answered, turning back to her mirror and taking up her sponge and cold-cream. "But not Fifi Glusac, ze world's premiere 'armonicist-contortionist."

"Which is why I'm here." He took another puff on the cigar and adjusted the angle of his fez. "Do you mind if I ask you a rather personal question?" he whispered, leaning closer to her.

"Providing it's got nozzing to do wiz zat report in ze *Egyptian Gazette* about moi and zat sheikh. Gosh, all I did was get into a double-lock half-twist with inverted elbows and my nose behind my kneecap while doing 'Somewhere Over ze Rainbow'. Next zing, he's offering me forty camels and a dozen oil rigs!"

"No, no, it's nothing to do with that. No, what I want to ask is: do you earn enough money out of your profession to make you really … *happy*?"

Fifi Glusac lowered her sponge and squinted at his reflected image. "Why do you ask?"

"Well, I happen to know that theatrical people are mostly dreadfully underpaid, and this seems a great shame, considering the wonderful work you all do. Why, mademoiselle, without the pretenders, the dreams of the ordinary people would be very flat. Wouldn't you agree?"

"Oui, oui."

"And I've always believed that people of your ilk

should be rewarded much more handsomely for the wonderful works you do. Money, as I have discovered, helps to buy happiness."

"You couldn't speak a truer word, buster. Oui, a few extra piastres every week wouldn't go to waste, believe moi."

"Oh, I could give you more than that! Much, much more than that! How does the thought of *rubies* grab you? Big, fat, glistening red gems that will—"

She stood again and swirled around to face him, her feathers gusting in her wake. "Okay, buster, zat's enough! I get you guys in 'ere all ze time, always offering moi jewels and chocolates and everyzing but ze kitchen sink – actually one chappie ran a plumbing empire, he offered me as many of *zem* as I wanted – and you all zink I'll fall for your sweet talking and your 'ollow promises and your sugary offers—"

"My offer is not sugary, mademoiselle, it is genuine. I plan to take artifice out of the theatre and into the real world where it will make me – and you as well, if you are agreeable – very comfortable indeed. With your help, I can obtain those rubies which, as we speak, are being kept at an isolated ancient site in the south-east of Mexico. I am, you see, one of the world's most pre-eminent archaeologists, and admirably experienced in the finding of ancient sites."

"Oh, oui?"

"I most certainly am." He blew a column of smoke into the air.

"Were you wiz zat group from ze Old Relics Society who saw ze show tonight?"

"No, La Stupenda, although I *am* one of the Society's more important members. No, all of those gentlemen out there tonight were *erstwhile* archaeologists and excavationists. Long retired. They're positively ancient themselves."

"Zat accounts for all zat denture-sucking," said Fifi, checking her curls in the mirror. "Slurp, slurp, slurp. Sometimes zey were sucking zeir dentures with such gusto I could barely 'ear myself blowing."

"Arrr. I" – he wiggled a hairy eyebrow in a superior fashion – "am still out in the field."

"You're big enough to *be* ze field," Fifi Glusac thought. But she kept her thought to herself and spoke instead. "I don't understand fully, Mr Zoomah—"

"Monty," he interrupted with a heavy-lidded wink.

"I don't understand what all of zis has got to do with moi." She began to absent-mindedly doodle on a sheet of writing paper with a stub of cumquat-coloured greasepaint. "I mean, why don't you just go on over to Mexico *yourself* if you know where zese rubies are, and grab 'em? Why do you need moi?"

The wedged-in man shifted uncomfortably in his chair and took from the pocket of his waistcoat a gold fob-watch on a rose-gold chain. He inspected the watch's dial with what Fifi Glusac (viewing him in the mirror as she doodled) thought was a look of restrained impatience. Then he looked once again at the entertainer.

"As I mentioned, it is a matter of *artifice*. In order to procure the rubies, I need the assistance of someone with particular natural qualities. *Specialised*, you might say. Unique. There is nobody else whom I know of who has these particular attributes. Nobody but the incomparable Mademoiselle Fifi Glusac."

She shut one eye and regarded him. "Hmmm. I'm still not convinced you're on ze—"

She stopped abruptly as a tinge of shadow swooped through the opened door. The shadow hovered for a brief moment before coming to settle atop the fez of Montgomery Zoomah.

Fifi Glusac turned. In the glow from the chandelier, she saw what this shadow was: a raven, with black-as-pitch, dull feathers and blood-red eyeballs that throbbed silently as the bird stared at her. Around its neck hung a thick coil of hessian rope, the bottom of the loop resting against the creature's pot belly.

It pecked at something on one of its wings – Fifi wasn't sure *what*, but whatever it was seemed to be troubling the raven, because of the ferocity of its pecking. Then it raised its head and opened its beak.

And spoke:

"Craaaark. Have you got her on side yet? That boat leaves in half an hour."

"I know, you feral flea-feathered felon," the man hissed.

"And 'oo," asked Fifi, "might *zis* be?"

Zoomah spoke quickly. "It *might* be Lassie, but it is

not. Allow me to introduce you to my assistant. Her name is Dessie."

The raven's eyeballs throbbed redly.

"Short for Desgusting," Zoomah added under his breath.

"Oh, isn't she cute?" gushed Fifi, a smile spreading across her heavily painted lips. "One zing I absolutely *adore* is feathers!"

"Cute?" The raven's beak seemed to curl in disgust. "*Cute?* Hecccchh! Listen, lady, I'm *despicable!*" There was a pride in her raspy voice when she spat the last word.

"No, I zink you're so *sweet*." Fifi sprang from her chair and went to caress a wing. "Petite Dessie, you—"

"*Scraaaarrrrrrk!*" The bird's beak took a savage snap at Fifi's fingers, which the harmonicist-contortionist quickly withdrew. "Nevermore, nevermore, nevermore!"

"Pardon!" gasped Fifi, shocked.

"It is best not to demonstrate affection towards her," advised Montgomery Zoomah. "Human beings are not on the list of her favourite things in life."

"Especially not *women* human beings," spat Dessie.

Fifi retired to her dressing table, hurt but not defeated.

"So," said Zoomah urgently, "will you accompany us to Mexico to obtain this glorious stash of wealth? Do you want to change your lifestyle for the better? How does the thought of a change of place and pace sound, not to mention the added thrill of jungle exotica and mystery?"

"You sound like an ad in a badly written tourist brochure, Mr Zoomah."

"*Monty*, Mademoiselle!"

"Crark, hurry up!"

"But I am afraid zat I need a little more … *persuasion*." She turned back to the mirror and smeared some cold-cream across her high cheekbones.

Montgomery Zoomah dropped his cigar to the floor and ground it with his heel into the rug. "Oh, there'll be lots of time for *that*," he whispered, rising to his feet. Taking a chloroform-soaked handkerchief from his pocket, he advanced towards her, and the raven uncurled the rope with diabolical pleasure.

2

A PEEK INTO THE PAST

"HERE YOU GO, Mr Jim, get a few of these into you. They will give your taste-buddies a thrill, I give you my words."

Cairo Jim, that well-known archaeologist and little-known poet, was sitting at a table under a palm tree in the open-air courtyard of the Amun-Ra Tea Rooms in Gurna village. He pushed back his pith helmet and stared at the plate of gaudy cakettes that had been put in front of him by Mrs Amun-Ra, the stout and friendly proprietress of this, his favourite establishment in Upper Egypt.

"Thank you, Mrs A," he smiled. "They look ... well ... goodness, they're *colourful*, aren't they?"

Mrs Amun-Ra clapped her hands together, causing a small cloud of baking flour to burst quietly out around her fingertips. "You won't find any more colourful pieces of pastry in the whole of Africa, I quarantine you. You would not believe how hard it is to get the purple and orange and pineapple and raspberry and tangerine and lime shades to sit in neat little rows like that and not run into each other. *That* would look like a dog's luncheon, I am sure."

"Yes, I suppose it would." Jim put on his special desert

sun-spectacles to protect his eyes from the brightness of the cakettes. He picked one up gingerly and was relieved when the abundance of colours did not smear all over his fingers. "I've never seen anything like it in all my travels."

"I am not surpassed you haven't," beamed Mrs Amun-Ra, pulling up a vacant chair and plonking herself into it. "It is a brand-new recipe, one that I have only just added for the first time to my menu. And, being my favourite archaeologist boyo, I thought that you should be my first taster."

"I'm honoured, Mrs A." Jim held the cakette before his mouth, trying to decide where to take the first bite. "What do you call them?"

"Striped Sphinxettes. I got the recipe from my dear sister, Tushratti. Oh, if you think *I* am a wonderful chef, you should taste *her* cooking. She could take a handful of weeds from the delta and whip up a meal fit for a Pharaoh. Her plump little macaroonies used to attract the admirers from as far away as Zarundi! She used to cook the most delectitious meals and pastries for her husband, you know. But alas, they are no longer together as a matter of fat."

Cairo Jim moved the unbitten Striped Sphinxette away from his mouth. "You mean a matter of *fact*, don't you, Mrs A?"

"No, Mr Jim, it was a matter of *fat*. Most definitively. He got so big from her cooking, there was not room enough for the two of them in the one house. So out he went."

"Oh," Jim said.

"The way of the worlds is a funny thing sometimes, don't you agree?"

He smiled and had another look at the Striped Sphinxette, and was just about to take a deep breath and wedge it into his mouth, all in one go (to get the experience of eating it over and done with), when the still air around them was suddenly broken by the flap-flap-flapping whoosh of wings.

They looked up to see the beautiful, graceful form of Cairo Jim's constant companion, the macaw named Doris, as she circled around the palm tree and glided effortlessly down to land on Jim's shoulder.

"Why, hello, my dear," Jim smiled, putting down the Striped Sphinxette quickly (but not ungraciously, he hoped). He reached up and tickled the small gold and blue feathers next to her beak.

"Greetings, salutations and whatnots," squawked Doris, opening her huge wings and folding them around her. "Gidday, Mrs A. Rark."

"Hello, Miss Doris. I was beginning to think you were not going to eventuate."

"My apologies," she blinked. "I would have been here earlier, but I got held up at camp. I'm having a bad feather day. Just washed them and can't do a thing—"

She laid her eyes on the plate full of Striped Sphinxettes and gave an immediate, ricocheting screech that made several of the other patrons of the Tea Rooms jump in alarm.

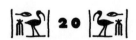

"*REEEEEERRRRRRAAAAAAAARRRRRRRKK KKKK!*"

Jim soothed her with his reassuring hand. "Steady on, Doris, don't get in a flap. They're only something new Mrs A's baked."

"Oh, you excitable thing." Mrs Amun-Ra shook her head. "Settle up. They are called Striped Sphinxettes."

Doris peered at them suspiciously. "You mean, you *cooked* them?"

"With my own two hands."

"Well that's all right, then. For a moment I thought they were a conspiracy of gaudy centipedes. They can give one a very nasty tummy if they nip you in the belly region."

"You cheeky bird, you," said Mrs Amun-Ra.

Jim held his arm up and Doris hopped onto it. Carefully he set her onto the table, next to the plate of cakettes. "So, where's Brenda?"* he asked her.

"Back at camp. Got her snout stuck in another of those Melodious Tex western adventure novels. *Melodious Tex and the Ghostly Guns of Gladiolus Gully*. Rark. She's over the hills and far away with that one. I tried to get her to come over, but she wouldn't budge. Don't know what she sees in that musical cowboy."

"Ah, it takes all sorts to make up the worlds," Mrs Amun-Ra said in her wisest tone.

---

* Brenda the Wonder Camel, the other of Cairo Jim's constant companions.

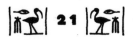

The macaw's small eyes narrowed and opened, and the feathers around them wrinkled. "'Full of most excellent differences, of very soft society and great showing'," she quoted. "*Hamlet,* by Mr Shakespeare, Act Five, Scene Two."

"Very good, Doris." Jim smiled and turned his thoughts back to the Striped Sphinxette, when Doris started hopping up and down.

"Has Miss Frith showed yet?" she squawked.

"No," answered Jim, glancing at his Cutterscrog Old Timers Archaeological Timepiece on his wrist. "But she shouldn't be too long." He turned to Mrs Amun-Ra. "We're due to meet her here this morning, Mrs A. She's got some photographs to show us of some of the ancient sites she's just visited in Mexico." He sighed at the enticing thought of faraway ruins, and wished that he, too, was once again exploring distant lands.

"Oh," gasped Mrs Amun-Ra. "That woman certainly gets aroundabout, does not she? I think it's very brave that she travels so much, considering all of her little allergicnesses. It must make it diffluent for her sometimes, the way her skin and sinuses react to things the way they do."

"She *is* one of the world's best archaeological photographers, though," said Jim. "I guess her sense of a job well done overrides any annoying insects or sunburn."

"Rerk," rerked Doris. "Or unpurified water or synthetic cushion covers or ballpoint pens or apricots or perfumes or kitchen cleansers or cacti or theatre auditoriums or tarantulas or glossy magazines or the ninth letter of the Greek alphabet or cranberry juice or lipstick or politicians whose names begin with—"

"Yes, Doris, we get the message." Jim patted her crest plumage gently.

"Still, I am glad that she is meeting the two of you here." Mrs Amun-Ra stood and smoothed down her big, floury apron. "I am proud that my little establishment is always the hubbub of activity. Now I go and serve those nuns who have just come in. They sure look like they need to wet their wimples. Enjoy your Sphinxettes, my dears."

She reached down, quickly tweaked Jim's cheeks and Doris's cheekfeathers, and ploughed off between the tables, chairs and customers.

The ringing of a bicycle bell wafted across the hot air. "Sounds like Miss Frith," muttered Jim.

"Over there," Doris screeched, pointing with her wing towards the small ferry and felucca dock at the edge of the Nile. "She's just ridden off the ferry."

Pyrella Frith, in long white skirt, long-sleeved osnaburg blouse (also white) and a broad-brimmed white straw hat with a white mosquito net hanging from it, was pedalling earnestly up the main street of Gurna village. In and out she weaved, past the few honking taxis and the few honking geese, around the donkeys that ambled carelessly across the road, swerving her bicycle here and there to avoid hitting the heat-affected tourists who were stumbling around and wondering where exactly they were and why they had come to Egypt and what the weather would be like in a cooler clime like Scandinavia.

Finally, without mishap, she skidded up to the low wall near the date palm under which Jim and Doris were waiting at their table. She threw her slender leg impatiently across the bike and leaned it against the wall (the bike, not her leg – it was not artificial). Then she unbuckled a large, flat satchel and, gripping it firmly under her arm, entered the courtyard.

Cairo Jim stood and Doris hop-fluttered up onto his shoulder.

"Jim, Doris," she greeted them in her usual breathless tone, "so sorry I'm late. Bit of a kerfuffle on the ferry. Some wretched tourist man thought I was his daughter and kept on trying to find out if I'd locked the front door to his yurt. Wouldn't believe that we weren't related. Then he started going on about the turnips. For heaven's sake, I mean, do I look like a woman who'd be interested in the cultivation of vegetables in Mongolia? I was so glad when the ferry finally docked, especially as the deluded man was showing the other passengers snapshots of a small baby with nothing on, lying on a yak-skin rug, and telling them it was yours truly."

"Yes, I understand," nodded Jim, "absolutely. Exactly the same thing happened to me last week. Here, Miss Frith, have a chair."

"Thank you." She sat gracefully but with purpose,

fanning her mosquito net with a small white lace handkerchief.

Jim and Doris sat, and Doris flexed herself up and down. "We're *dying* to see your photos," she cooed.

"Death is the extreme to which we all must succumb," Pyrella Frith remarked in her quietly philosophical manner as she began to untie the cord around her satchel. "But have no fear, you enthusiastic bird, I shall certainly show you my latest images during your lifetime. Oh, there are things here that will make your pith helmet wobble, Cairo Jim! Feast your desert sun-spectacles on these!"

With a flourish of her thin, cotton-gloved fingers she spread a series of large colour photographs across the table, almost upsetting the plate of Striped Sphinxettes in the process. "These wall and floor paintings are quite remarkable, and only just discovered."

Jim and Doris leaned forward, scrutinising the photographs carefully. For several minutes they neither said nor squawked a word.

"Well, smear me with paint and call me a fresco," Jim whispered at last. "Miss Frith, they're beautiful."

"Not recently have I seen such a woman 'with colours fairer painted'," Doris muttered, quoting in part from *The Tempest*.

"Nor I, Doris," smiled Pyrella. "Nor I…"

"They're so well preserved," commented Jim. "The colours may have faded, I'll grant that, but they're still beautiful."

The colours of the images of the painted woman were indeed beautiful in their paleness: faint amber for her skin; jade-green ornaments hanging from her ears and in her nose; light orange on her fingernails. Her lips were a dim crimson, her eyes (which were slightly crossed) a subtle mauve and she wore a tunic of dull apricot that was trimmed with an ochre border, which itself was decorated with stripes and checks and geometric patterns.

Sometimes she was standing against a background of deep, but faded, green; at other times it was gentle blue or a soft peach colour.

But the most strikingly colourful area on all of the photographs was around the woman's head. Rising from her dark hair, and then flowing like a cascade of water down the shoulders of her tunic, was a grand, vibrant headdress made up entirely of shimmering green-blue feathers. This was always the most unfaded area on each photo.

Jim hadn't seen feathers that long in quite a while. "Miss Frith," he whispered, "are they … are they *quetzal* feathers?"

"Rark," flapped Doris, blinking her small eyes. "Certainly look like 'em to me."

"I'd say they are," answered Pyrella. She slapped at an insect that was buzzing perilously close to the gap between her mosquito net and her neck. "It's the ancient bird of nobility in Mexico, after all."

Jim fiddled with the brim of his pith helmet, pushing

it up onto his brow and then pulling it down again. "Who is she, do you think?" he asked.

"That we don't know."

"I've never seen any similar images of her in my travels. Nor in any of the books up in the Old Relics Society library in Cairo."

"Me neither," Doris chirped in.

"And she's a bolt out of the blue to me as well," said Pyrella. "The archaeologists I was working for in Mexico also couldn't place her. It seems no one's ever seen her before. They've christened her 'The Quetzal Queen' until we find out who she *really* was."

"Well, swoggle me secretively," Jim said. "Tell me, at which site did you photograph her? Is she an Aztec ruler or Mayan or Toltec or what?"

"Now *that*," Pyrella beamed, "is the *really* intriguing part." She stopped for a moment until all eyes were on her instead of the faded woman from the past. "Jim, you don't happen to have your Broad Horizons Archaeological Expandable Atlas on you at the moment, do you?"

"In my knapsack," answered the archaeologist-poet, leaning down and rummaging about underneath the table. "I never leave the tent without it. Here we are." He placed the small, brown, leather-covered book onto the table.

"Open it to Mexico," instructed Pyrella. "A complete country map if you have one."

Jim did so and, turning his wrist and gripping the

corner of the map, gently pulled out the entire landscape of Mexico until it had expanded and covered the tabletop of photographs and Striped Sphinxettes. (They were lying under the mountainous regions around Mexico City, so the bulges in the map didn't look too out of place.)

"Now the really intriguing part is this." Pyrella moved her white-gloved hand slowly across the map. "The paintings weren't just found in the *one* site."

"No?"

"Rark?"

"No, they were found at *several* ancient locations. Look, here, close to Mexico City, on the top of the Pyramid of the Sun at Teotihuacán. There they found the painting of her against the peach-coloured background. Another was found inside the top of the Temple of Inscriptions at Palenque, alongside the carvings of the great King Pakal."

"About seven hundred and sixty kilometres from Teotihuacán," Jim observed. "It's jungle territory there."

"The next one – the image of the Quetzal Queen standing in front of the blue background – was discovered at Chichén Itzá, inside the temple at the top of the Pyramid of Kukulcán. Right by the northern staircase, if you want to be precise. I don't mind telling you I was a bit puffed getting up all those steps on that very hot day, what with all my cameras and equipment. I was tempted to leave some of the heavier stuff at the bottom, but didn't. A woman should never be without her tripods, I always say."

"Not to mention her spare rolls of film," Doris squawked. "You never know what might develop! Ha-crark-ha!"

"Very funny, Doris." Pyrella rolled her eyes beneath her veil.

"Hmm," hmmed Cairo Jim, studying the map intently. "Chichén Itzá's about five hundred and twenty kilometres from Palenque. This Quetzal Queen certainly got around, didn't she?"

"Absolutely," nodded Pyrella Frith. "She was more widespread than yoghurt." She gave a tiny shudder which went unnoticed by Jim or Doris – yoghurt was yet another allergy. "The last painting is inside the crowning temple of the Pyramid of the Magician at Uxmal, a few hours' drive in an adequate vehicle from Chichén Itzá. This is the finest painting of her; her quetzal plumes almost seem to waft off the very walls!"

"Rark!" Doris opened and closed her majestic wings and blinked thrice. "I'm flabbergasted to my follicles."

"What about you, Jim? Is it impressive enough for a seasoned archaeologist such as yourself?"

Jim didn't answer straight away. He sat there, staring at the map, all of his senses floating in and around and above and below him, as the mighty realisations of all he had just heard and seen and figured began to settle on him like a huge, electrifying feather.

"Jim? You still with us?"

"Rark? Anyone home?" Doris hopped onto his shoulder and pecked him lightly on the pith helmet.

He took off his sun-spectacles and eased them into one of the pockets on his shirt. "I've just realised two things of the most extraordinary magnitude," he said, his voice hardly audible.

"Yes?" asked Pyrella.

Doris flexed her wings and prerked impatiently. "Spill the beans!"

Which is exactly what he did.

3

COLOURFUL REALISATIONS

"FIRSTLY," explained Jim, trying to keep his voice quietly controlled in spite of the surge of excitement that was accosting his vocal chords, "the Quetzal Queen is absolutely unique. Why, as far as we've discovered to date, she is the *only* ruler from ancient Mexico's cultures *whose likeness has been found at more than one site!*"

"Rerark, hang onto your camels for a minute, Jim." Doris hopped back onto the map and began to flex up and down in her plumpish, waddling manner. "How about Chac, for instance? The Mayan Rain God? Didn't I read in one of the books in the Old Relics Society's library that there are carved masks of him at *lots* of ancient sites on the Yucatán peninsula?"

"Yes, my dear, you probably did. There *are* many images of Chac around. But he was a god, not a mortal ruler. There are lots of depictions of the *gods* of old Mexico, at many different sites. But not of the human kings and – here for the first time, it seems – *queens* who controlled the great empires. Each area had its own sovereign, and it was only that king's or queen's likeness, and that likeness alone, that ever appeared in the temples and palaces and pyramids of that particular sovereign's region. Look at the vast distances where the

Quetzal Queen's greatness was felt. She must've reigned across almost the whole of Mexico."

"What a Queen!" Doris squawked, hopping about as though her tailfeathers were on fire.

"You bet," said Jim.

"How do we know for certain that she was human?" enquired Pyrella. "Maybe she was a god, like Chac?"

"Ah, no. Those earrings and nose decorations she's wearing in your photos were only ever worn by royalty. The gods were never shown with such adornment. They never needed it, I guess. And her headdress would also be symbolic of the status of a member of the ruling classes."

A small breeze wafted across from the river Nile, gently ruffling Pyrella's insect veil and puffy cotton sleeves. "How amazing," she breathed, her veiled eyes flickering with admiration for this man of unceasing (yet modest) knowledge. "And the second thing of extraordinary magnitude? What's that, Jim?"

Cairo Jim took a long, deep breath. "I think we've stumbled upon some phenomenally swoggling piece of history here … a piece of history, a *riddle* of history, if you like … that up until now we've never been aware of."

"Rark, what?"

Jim put the fingertips of both his hands to his temples and began to massage slowly. "It's almost so overwhelming I feel like I'm dreaming. Listen. At Teotihuacán, where the first Quetzal Queen painting was found, the Pyramid of the Sun dates to around 150 AD. The next site, Palenque, was at its height between

615 and 683 AD – that's when Pakal was the King. The Pyramid of Kukulcán at Chichén Itzá was built before 800 AD, and we know that Uxmal, the fourth place where the Queen has appeared, was abandoned by about 900 AD."

"Very good," flapped the macaw. "You know your dates. But what's all that got to do with the price of eggheads?"

"My dear, dear Doris." Jim stopped massaging his temples and put his hand on her crest. "All of those buildings were built over a period of about seven hundred and fifty years. Seven hundred and fifty years! Maybe even longer. They've found the image of the Quetzal Queen in *all* of those places. That means, my dear—"

"*Waaaarrrrrccckkk!*" Doris slapped a wing across her beak and her eyes grew wide.

"Well snap me candidly," gasped Pyrella Frith.

"*That means that the Quetzal Queen must have reigned over her people for at least seven hundred and fifty years. The longest reign of any human monarch that the world has ever seen!*"

For a few minutes they were all as silent as stones, while the information began to sink in. An invisible curtain of stunnedness hung above them.

Then Jim politely brushed Doris to one side of the table and began to refold the map of Mexico until it was a small, compact oblong that fitted neatly into his Broad Horizons Archaeological Expandable Atlas.

"But how?" asked Pyrella, after the map was stashed away in its rightful place. "How could she have reigned for such a long, long time?"

"Search me," Doris blinked.

Jim looked down at the beautifully mottled and faded colours in Pyrella Frith's photographs, and then across at the bright, glaring colours of Mrs Amun-Ra's Striped Sphinxettes. In the late afternoon haze, as his eyes filled with a liquid tingle of great excitement, the colours seemed to converge.

"I wonder," he said, "if we'll ever know how she could have reigned for seven hundred and fifty years." His heart began tugging at his wouldn't-it-be-perfect-to-go-abroad tendons, deep in his chest. "But how I'd *love*, more than anything right now, to try and find out," he sighed wistfully.

4

SNAILWORK AND SKULKING

FORTUNE LEANED A LITTLE the next day, in the way that Fortune sometimes does lean when you wish passionately for a thing to happen.

Gerald Perry Esquire, Cairo Jim's wealthy patron and financier of all Jim's expeditions and diggings (not to mention one of the Founding Members of the Old Relics Society in Cairo), had placed an early morning call to Jim on the archaeologist-poet's field telephone at the trio's camp in the Valley of the Kings. Jim, Doris and Brenda the Wonder Camel must come at once to Society headquarters, Perry had urged. There was a mystery that he had stumbled upon; one that he needed to confer with Jim about.

So it was that by five-fifteen the next morning, Jim had saddled Brenda with her ornate macramé saddle, and Doris had flapped around a bit at having to wake up at so uncivilised an hour, screeching in a gravelly sort of way for a while and blinking her small eyes as though this time of the day was an insult to her very existence, and Jim had soothed her feathers and whispered praiseworthy things to her until she had settled down and cooed that yes, she *was* a noble bird after all, one who would thrive on a morning of early

activity that was surely a break from their usual routine, and then Jim and Doris had mounted Brenda and, casting a quick but observant eye over their camp, Jim had prodded the beautiful Wonder Camel gently with the heel of his boot and they had all departed north for Cairo.

As the sands whirled around her pounding hoofs, Brenda's heart beat in time to the rhythm of her steady pace. Her beautifully groomed mane tingled with the pleasure of having her two favourite beings on her back – Jim straight-spined and erect in the saddle, Doris sitting forward on the pommel. For the two-humped beast of breathtaking beauty, all was right with the world when man, bird and beast were on the same road.

"Rerark," squawked Doris after a few hours. "What d'you reckon Perry wants, Jim?"

"Didn't say," shouted Jim over the sound of the wind and tiny grains of sand that were blasting steadily against his face. "Just told me there was something very grave he wished to discuss, and that we were to get up there as soon as possible."

"Quaaooo," snorted Brenda, her nostrils flaring with the urgency of her task. "You'll be there *sooner* than possible," she thought in her telepathic way. "Or I'm not a Wonder Camel!"

"But," hollered Jim, "at this rate we'll be there *sooner* than possible. Or Brenda's not a Wonder Camel!"

"Rark," squawked Doris in agreement.

★　　★　　★

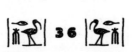

Shortly after ten o'clock Brenda clattered up the marble stairs at the front of the Old Relics Society in Talaat Harb Street and, swerving between the cream-coloured granite pillars gleaming in the bright morning sun, she hurtled into the immense building and skidded to a halt at the huge mahogany reception bureau.

The squeal of her hoofs scraping against the marble floor echoed through the enormous foyer like a hundred sets of fingernails going down a blackboard.

"Ooooooh," winced Spong, the Old Relics Society Receptionist and Hat-and-Walking-Aid-Checker-Inner. His pale hands shot to his ears and his paler eyes rolled backwards into his head. "Cairo Jim and company. It's been" – Spong gulped, took his hands from his ears and rolled his eyes back to normal – "it's been a *while* since you were last here, hasn't it?"

"That it has," replied Jim, dismounting and patting Brenda firmly and appreciatively on the side of her neck. "Good to see you, Spong."

"I'm glad for you," Spong said.

Brenda moved her hoofs along the floor, trying to find a stance that wasn't too skiddy. Another, shorter squeal shot out. Spong quickly crossed his eyes and uncrossed them again, hoping that Jim wouldn't see him doing this and that the silent action might avert some of the noise from entering his eardrums fully.

It didn't.

"Having those awful headaches still?" Jim asked.

"Yes, it's that time of the year again." Spong shook

his head and inserted one finger into an ear, jiggling it around a bit.

"Skwerk!" Doris skwerked. "We're here to find Gerald Perry Esquire."

"Yes," Jim said. "Any idea where he might be?"

Brenda's hoofs squealed once more and Spong pulled a face that was exactly the same face he had pulled when he was a child and had drunk an entire bottle of castor oil very quickly on a very hot day, in the mistaken belief that it was chilled lemonade.

"Careful," Jim warned, "if you do that for too long your face'll turn inside out."

"Mr Perry, when last I saw him," muttered Spong through gritted teeth, "was lurking behind the left heel of the feet of King Raneferef."*

"Thank you," said Jim. He took Brenda by the bridle and, with Doris perched on his shoulder, led them off to the feet of King Raneferef in the corner of the huge vestibule. "Hope your head clears soon."

Brenda's parting hoof-squeal made Spong jump so swiftly that he left his shoes behind.

The trio approached the enormous stone feet, trying to spy Gerald Perry Esquire.

---

* Two gigantic carved feet of the Pharaoh Raneferef (2418–2408 BC), discovered – without the rest of the statue – in 1932 and taken to the Old Relics Society, where they are still on display in the entry vestibule.

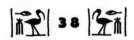

"I think Spong's playing tricks," Doris said. "There's no one round them tootsies at all."

"Look by the ankle," thought Brenda with a small snort.

"Let's look by the ankle," Jim said, picking up on her idea.

Sure enough, there by the bump that was the left foot's ankle, they found the crouching figure of Perry.

"Perry!" called Jim, extending his hand.

"Go away you, I told you before I don't want to look at your snail shells, not today or ... oh." Gerald Perry's eyes settled on Cairo Jim and twinkled. "Jim! You're here at last. Morning, Doris. Morning, Brenda."

"Reerrk!"

"Quaaaooo!"

"Snail shells?" asked Jim.

"Mmm," frowned Perry. With a slight struggle he straightened himself and leaned against the mighty ankle. "I'm hiding. Trying to avoid that Binkie Whiskin."

"Why?"

Perry looked furtively around. "Because the confounded old chappie wants to show me his snail-shell collection. He's got over four-and-a-half thousand of 'em! Four-and-a-half thousand!"

"That's a lot of snail shells," said Cairo Jim.

"For the love of Hetepheres, they're not even *exotic* snail shells, just the common garden variety. Drab and dull as dishwater, and all the same as each other if y'ask me. Last man he showed 'em to got so bored he went to sleep for three days solid in the Society clubroom. They had to wake him by shoving corks up his nostrils."

"Snails, hmmm?" prowled Doris.

"Don't you worry, you opportunistic macaw. There're no snails in the shells for you to eat. No, old Binkie Whiskin had *those* removed years ago. Gosh, he's so absorbed by snail shells he could write an encyclopaedia about 'em." Perry rubbed his moustache this way and that. "Come to think of it, he *has* written an encyclopaedia. Forty-eight volumes to be exact. *The Joy of Snail Shells*."

"I see," said Jim.

"Not that I'd ever take 'em off the shelves to read. Why, I'd rather have m'head stuck in a tuba than—"

"You wanted to see us?" flapped Doris, trying to get things back on track.

"Mmm? Oh, yes, so I did. Good of you to come up at such short notice. Let's go somewhere quiet, where Binkie Whiskin won't find us, and I'll tell you all about why I summoned you."

"Rightio."

Perry crouched low once again and looked in all directions. "Hmmph," he said. "Look at that man Spong up there, hanging from the chandelier. Does he think we pay him to spend all day swinging on the light fittings? I'll have a word to the other Members about *him*, you see if I don't! Now come on, follow me to the library. I know a suitably gloomy corner where no one ever goes."

And off he led them, like a scuttling crab in a white linen suit.

Down the cool and dim corridors they went, Brenda being grateful that they had all moved off the marble floors and onto the wooden parquetry, which gave her hoofs better grip.

Presently, after Perry had led them around many corners and had made them press themselves close to the walls on a few occasions whenever he thought he could hear the approaching footsteps of Binkie Whiskin ("I'd know the sound of that man's footsteps anywhere," Perry had whispered, "he even *walks* like a snail!"), they hurried into the Old Relics Society's huge library. With light footsteps, hoofsteps and low-turbulence fluttering they hurried to the suitably gloomy corner where no one ever went.

"Have a seat," Perry gestured, lowering himself into one of the two plump leather armchairs behind a tall shelf of cobwebbed and musty books that hadn't been borrowed in at least forty years.

Jim did likewise, and Doris hop-fluttered onto Jim's chair's arm. Brenda clamped her nostrils tightly shut to avoid getting the dust from the forgotten books in her snout.

"Now, what's all this about?" asked Cairo Jim, taking off his pith helmet and looking curious.

Perry clasped his hands in his lap and leaned forward. "How would you all like a little trip down to Mexico?"

Jim's heart skipped the tiniest of beats, Doris's feathers ruffled in the tiniest of ways and Brenda's eyelashes tingled with the tiniest of zinginess.

Jim was so excited his poetry cells welled up, and before he knew it he was blurting:

> "If thirsting in the desert,
> we'd found oasis blue,
> it would be nought compared beside
> the timeliness of you,
> for you're our benefactor,
> the strawberries to our cream,
> the one who gives us all the chance
> to travel and to dream!"

"Rerk," Doris squawked, screwing up her beak.

Gerald Perry squirmed in his chair. "A simple 'Yes, Perry, I'd love to' would have been sufficient," he said.

(But Brenda didn't mind her friend's outburst and snorted quietly with approval.)

"Perry, we'd love to, wouldn't we, gang?"

"Yep," Doris said, and Brenda rolled her head and neck in a wide circular movement.

"It'll mean we can get a chance to have a look for ourselves at the extraordinary wall paintings of the Quetzal Queen. We've just seen Pyrella Frith's pictures. Do you know, Perry, I think she might've reigned for at least seven hundred and fifty years? The Quetzal Queen, not Pyrella Frith. I'd sure love to get to the bottom of her—"

"Eh?" Perry pulled a shocked face.

"Her *mystery*. The Quetzal Queen's, not Pyrella Frith's."

"Just a minute, Jim. I'm not sending you to Mexico for any Quetzal Queen, even if she *has* got a mysterious bottom."

"Oh?" Jim looked puzzled, and the beginnings of disappointment started to curl into his eyebrows.

"Nope," Perry shook his head slowly, "I'm afraid this is a little bit more personal than archaeology. Although of course if you get the chance, you *can* go and take a peek at the Queen. Time permitting, of course. No, this is most worrying."

He reached into the inside pocket of his blazer and took out a folded newspaper, which he opened up and spread across his knees. "Get a load of *that*," he said gravely.

Jim, Doris and Brenda leaned forward and Jim read out loud: "'MAN ACCIDENTALLY SWALLOWS WHEELBARROW.'"

"Reeeerk!" reeeerked Doris, flexing and closing her wings uncomfortably.

"Eh?" said Perry, looking carefully at the newspaper. "No, not that bit, the story underneath!"

"Oh." Jim turned his attention to the next headline. "'FAMOUS ARTISTE DISAPPEARS … HARMONICIST-CONTORTIONIST MISSING

FOR TEN DAYS.'" Jim looked up at Perry.

"Go on, keep reading," Perry urged.

"'Mademoiselle Fifi Glusac, the world's most celebrated simultaneous mouth-organ player and contor-tionist, is being sought by detectives of the Entertainers Division of the Cairo Police Force. Mlle Glusac has been missing for the past ten days. Police say she was last seen leaving the Cairo Gaiety Theatre after her evening performance on 15 April and she has not reported for further performances since. It is believed that foul play in the form of kidnapping may be on the agenda.

"'Anyone with information regarding Mlle Glusac's whereabouts should contact Inspector Boutros Boutros Sateen, Entertainers Division, Cairo Police. A reward will be paid handsomely and with flair.'"

Doris moved her neck quickly up and down. "And what, pray tell, has all of this got to do with us?"

"More to the point," said Jim, "what's it got to do with *you*, Perry?"

Perry squirmed again in his chair.

"You don't know where she *is*, do you?" Jim asked.

"Eh? Me? No, no, of course not! That's why I asked you lot to come and help. I'm worried half to the After Life about her, if you want t'know the truth of it."

"Rark! So you *know* this Fifi Glusac then?" Doris fixed him with a beady eye.

"Most certainly I do. I've been a fan of hers ... no, I think I'd go as far as to say I've been a *devotee* of hers ... since she first started tangling on the boards." His eyes grew misty and he sighed wistfully. "There's none that can contort like Fifi Glusac, and I've seen 'em all! Speaking as a regular patron of the arts, of course."

"Of course," nodded Jim.

"Y'see, I used to know her father. He was a likeable man, old Randolph. Used to own an artificial-elbow factory that exported to Mogadishu and Tasmania, did very well out of it too, which surprised us all. Well, before old Randolph left us to go on to Bigger and Unforeseen Things, I made a promise to him that I'd keep an eye on Fifi. Make sure she didn't get herself into any scrapes or discombobulated positions she couldn't get herself out of."

"You mean, you're a sort of benefactor to her? Like you are to us?"

"You could look at it like that, Jim," Perry answered with a slight blush. "I've kept her in feathers – which she has a passion for – and liniments – which she has a need for – ever since."

Doris made a kind of disapproving, clucking noise; *she* didn't need any man to keep *her* in feathers.

"Anyway," continued Perry, "as her sort of unofficial guardian I take it upon m'self to look in on her performance regularly. Often organise little groups of the other Old Relics Society Members to have an outing and come along to be thrilled by her mellifluous dexterity. They especially like it when she puts her big toes into her ears and plays 'Don't Fence Me In', but the thing they like best is when she arches over backwards and does a soulful rendition of 'Roll Out the Barrel' with—"

"Yes, yes," said Jim, "but what do you know about her disappearance?"

"Ah." Perry's eyes lost their wistfulness and became worried. "I think I've discovered a few things those detectives haven't. And I think she *might*'ve been kidnapped!"

"Quaaaooo!" snorted Brenda, urging him on.

"Well, a few nights after she stopped turning up to the theatre, I went to see her perform, not knowing that she *hadn't* been performing. There was a big sign up out the front that said: 'THE MANAGEMENT OF THE CAIRO GAIETY THEATRE REGRETS THAT MADEMOISELLE FIFI GLUSAC IS INDISPOSED. GRAB A SNACK AT PERRY'S TAKEAWAY PIGEON RESTAURANTS AFTER THE SHOW!'. I do a little advertising there for m'restaurants, you understand."

"Yes, yes," said Doris impatiently.

"Now, when I found out that Fifi ... er, Mademoiselle Glusac ... wasn't going to be appearing that evening, I got a bit worried. She hadn't called me to tell me, you see. She normally *does* call me when she's not going to be performing, usually if she's got a bad cold or a headache or her leg stuck around her neck or something. That only happened *once*, mind you."

"Yes, yes," said Cairo Jim.

"So I ducked round the back of the theatre, to the Stage Door where I know the Stage Doorman ... er, a friend of a friend ... and let myself into Mademoiselle Glusac's dressing room. She'd given me a key to it, she had, just in case she got locked into some inextricable position and couldn't come to open the door if

I knocked." Perry tried to loosen his collar from his perspiring neck with his index finger.

"And?" Doris flarped.

"Well, inside that dressing room all was not right. There was powder all over the floor, and a few feathers strewn about. I guess they came off her clothes; she likes feathers sewn on her clothes."

"Hmmph," Doris hmmphed.

Perry pulled his handkerchief from his trousers and earnestly mopped his brow. "There'd obviously been some sort of a struggle in there, if you ask me. All of her harmonicas were scattered about, which was most unlike her. She always packed 'em up, straight away after her performance – um, so I read in some magazine or other."

"But what really led me to believe that she's been kidnapped is *this*." He reached into his blazer again and took out a small plastic envelope. He opened this and carefully slid from it a sheet of pale pink writing paper which had been folded several times.

"I didn't want to pass this on to the Entertainers Division; those police can be awfully slow to act on information like this, 'specially if it's pink." With gentle fingers he unfolded the sheet of paper and handed it to Jim.

The archaeologist-poet read the cumquat-coloured writing that looked like it had been done with a thick crayon.

"That's greasepaint, Jim," Perry advised. "And it's Fifi's ... er, Mademoiselle Glusac's ... handwriting."

"'M. ZOOMAH, ARCHAEOLOGIST,'" Cairo Jim read out loud. "'SOUTH-EAST MEXICO. FAT RED RUBIES. WHAT'S HE AFTER?'"

"Y'see?" Perry squealed. "She was suspicious!"

"Rark!" Doris squinted her beady eyes and carefully inspected the handwriting. "Looks very messy."

"Like it was done in a hurry," thought Brenda the Wonder Camel.

"Like it was done in a hurry," pondered Jim. "M. Zoomah, archaeologist. Hmm. Ever heard of him, Perry?"

"Can't say I have. I've been swirling the name around in m'head ever since I found the note. I checked the Society's Membership Papyrus; can't find a trace of him."

Doris flapped her wings. "Sounds like he's grabbed her, all right. Reeeerrraaaaarrrk!"

"When do you want us to leave?" Jim asked urgently.

"How about right now?" Perry once again reached into his blazer and produced a long, flat leather folder. "I've chartered you a small Valkyrian Airways aeroplane with a pilot and all. Here're the tickets and some Mexican pesos. And here" – he reached into another pocket and lovingly extricated a black-and-white theatrical photograph – "here is the artiste herself. So you know the beauty you're searching for. Not many around who can hold a harmonica between their elbows like that and scratch their heels at the same time!"

"Thank you, Perry. We'll jump to it."

"Rerk," rerked Doris, peering at the slightly cross-eyed Mademoiselle Fifi Glusac for the first time.

"She looks familiar, somehow."

"As all great and classical beauty does," sighed Gerald Perry Esquire. He blushed and quickly added, "Or so the poets tell us, of course."

"Of course," nodded Cairo Jim diplomatically.

5

VILLAINY AFLOAT

IN THE ONLY PASSENGER CABIN of a small, grimy cargo freighter ship, a large, fleshy man was pondering his substantial place in the universe.

The ship rolled and lurched as it ploughed slowly across the North Atlantic Ocean towards Mexico, but Captain Neptune Bone, the most unfinancial archaeologist ever to be a Member of the Old Relics Society, hardly felt the motion at all. His huge girth was wedged into a plush but slightly tatty armchair, the kind with high, rounded arms that seem to almost swallow you up.

His beefy legs – covered to the knees in a pair of geranium-coloured brocade plus-fours trousers, and from knees to ankles in long cashmere leggings decorated with tiny woven lemons and bananas – were splayed out in front of him. His ball-like ankles were crossed and his fatty feet, encased in their black-and-white spats, were resting on the top of an upright, lacklustre travelling trunk.

In between his thick lips a cigar was clamped, its thick and pungent smoke curling up, where it passed through his beard and moustache and came to linger around the horsehair tassel on his burgundy-coloured fez.

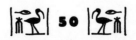

"Arrr," he murmured happily to himself while he gently and lovingly buffed his fingernails with a small silver fingernail buffer that was padded with the finest chamois leather. "Sometimes my ambition and daringness – those things that are mere portions of my innate greatness – are such that they overwhelm even me."

The port-hole by the door swung open and a smudge of dark feathers swooped into the cabin, coming to land on the top of the travelling trunk. Desdemona the raven shook out her dull, black-as-pitch feathers, and a deluge of seawater and fleas showered out and onto Bone's spats.

"You frightful flustration of feathers!" shrieked Bone, quickly uncrossing his feet and aiming a savage kick at the bird, who hopped speedily out of the way. "How dare you defile my grandeur?"

"Craaaark! Did I hear correctly?" Desdemona's eyes throbbed the colour of blood. "Did you say your greatness overwhelms you?"

Bone took the cigar from his mouth and flicked the ash at her. "I most certainly did. There is nothing wrong with spouting truths while at sea, you know. A man could do far worse."

"Truths? Ha-crark-ha. You being great has about as much truth to it as a salty marshmallow."

"Does not my greatness overwhelm *you*?"

"It did once, when you accidentally sat on me that time," she rasped. "Boy, I was so *overwhelmed*

I could've fitted into a pop-up toaster and—"

"*Enough*, Desdemona! Stop your complaining and enjoy our voyage into the bright and beckoning future. Into the rest of my glorious life."

The raven rolled her eyeballs and spoke to him as though he was a very stupid mollusc. "Tell me something, you great big non-reality zone. How do you expect me to *enjoy* myself when we're stuck in the middle of the ocean, heading back to Mexico for the umpteenth time? One trip to Mexico would be enough for most men, but not you. Oh, no, we've been there so many times now the Customs people just wave us through. They don't even bother to look at our passports!"

"A good thing too, seeing as how we don't possess any."

"Mexico, Mexico, Mexico! You know how I hate all those re-fried beans. They make me go all gooey and *that*" – she whipped out her tongue and licked up a flea from her belly – "I do *not* like. But here you are, telling me to enjoy myself. Sheesh."

"Enjoy the proximity of my greatness then, you queer quotation of quackiness." He put the cigar back between his teeth and spoke in a bold, actor-like voice in time to the buffing strokes on his fingernails: "Some are born with greatness; some of us have it rippling through every pore of our bodies. Arrr."

"With *your* body it'd be more of a *tidal wave* than a ripple. Old tsunami tummy, that's you, all right!"

"I'd take a swipe at you if you weren't so unswipable already."

She rose to her full height and fixed him with a beady eye. "You're deluded, that's what you are. Here I am being dragged all the way to the other end of the world, and for what?"

"You tell me, birdbrain."

"For a handful of rubies! Ha-crark-ha. A handful of measly rubies that'll probably get us enough money on the black market to keep us in cigars and tinned Japanese seaweed for three days. What a waste!"

"I can't bear the taste of tinned Japanese seaweed," sneered Bone.

"I was thinking of myself!" she spat.

Bone's lips curled into a wide grin of flabbiness. Slowly, from deep within his oversized chest, he began to chuckle.

"What are you chuckling about?"

He laid the fingernail buffer in his canyon of a lap, withdrew the cigar from his mouth and was about to answer her when there came a loud and angry rapping from inside the travelling trunk.

"'Allo, 'allo? Can you 'ear me?"

"We can hear you all right, Mademoiselle Glusac," leered Bone.

"Unfortunately," crowed Desdemona, smacking the top of the trunk sharply with her beak.

"Zat's La Stupenda, *si'l vous plaît*!" came the muffled voice. "It's dark in 'ere, you let moi out!"

"Not until you have a little think about our venture."

Bone puffed smarmily on the cigar, blowing the smoke at Desdemona. "It'll make things so much easier for us all if you come along with us, and *go* along with us, *willingly*."

The raven gave a sort of cough-belch and then, for the sheer pleasure of it, smacked the trunk sharply again with her beak.

"You cut that out! I can't breathe in 'ere, M'sieur Zoomah. *Si'l vous plaît*, let moi out!"

"Our baggage needs oxygen, Desdemona. I shall aerate your environs for you, Mademoiselle, and you must be content with that much of my generosity for the time being." He raised his hairy eyebrows at the raven. "Go on, you bothersome bundle of bilge, give La Stupenda a taste of your choppers."

"Crarrrk!" Desdemona didn't need to be asked a second time. She raised her head high and, in the swishest of instants, sliced her beak through the air, embedding the tip of her beak in the travelling trunk.

"Ooh!" squealed Fifi Glusac. "What do you zink I am, a magician's assistant or somezing? Careful wiz zat dagger, buster!"

Desdemona pulled her beak free, like a jagged saw being levered from a tough old log, and repeated the performance until there were four large breathing holes stabbed across the top of the trunk. It looked like the luggage had been sprayed with bullet-fire from an elephant-sized machine gun.

"*Si'l vous plaît*," implored Fifi, "it's cramped in 'ere! Let moi come out!"

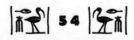

"That's enough out of you," snapped Bone. He replaced his feet (which he had hurriedly pulled out of the way during Desdemona's aerating activity) over most of the breathing holes. "It's a good thing she's a contortionist," he sneered.

"The first sensible thing you've said all night," agreed Desdemona. She prised some small splinters of timber out of the end of her beak. "You still haven't told me," she whined, "why we're going to all this trouble for a mere handful of rubies? What's the game, Captain?"

"Game?" he asked in an insulted voice. "You think that I, the genius who single-handedly discovered ChaCha Muchos, the Lost City of the Dancers—"

"Ha! You fell in the water!"

"I, who took the Sacred Alabastron of Cronus to the mysterious island of Samothraki—"

"Har! You fell in the water!"

"I, who located the fabled sunken golden sarcophagus of the Pharaoh Sekheret—"

"Harr! You got *lost* in the water!"

"I, who found the missing tomb of Pharaoh Martenarten—"

"And was pile-driven into the sand!"

"Do you think that I am going to all of this trouble in order to play a little *game*?"

"It seems like a ridiculous way to kill time, if you ask me. Going all across the globe and back again like headless chooks, all for the sake of a few pathetic little rubies."

"Killing time? Pathetic little rubies?" The large man's belly started to wobble and his cheeks began turning red under his beard. "Do you think I would be *killing time* going after a piddling collection of rubies?" He lowered his voice to a rumbling whisper:

"No, no, no, Desdemona, there are no rubies; what I'm looking for is far greater than *that*. If I find it, I shall be able to do much more than *kill time*. I shall be able to *injure the very bounds of Eternity! Aaaaarrrrrrr!*"

And he threw back his head and laughed like a hurricane about to wreak catastrophic havoc.

6

AN ANCIENT DIVERSION

THREE DAYS LATER, after a turbulence-free flight on the Valkyrian Airways plane that Perry had hired, Cairo Jim and Doris were hanging on tightly to Brenda the Wonder Camel as she hurtled through the early evening's dimming glimmer and out of Mexico City.

"Jim!" screeched Doris, riding on Jim's pith helmet after they had left the tall buildings of the city behind.

"Yes, my dear?" he shouted back, above the noise of Brenda's thundering hoofs.

"One question. Rark. In which direction are we headed?"

The archaeologist-poet reached down into Brenda's saddlebag and into his knapsack (being careful not to lose his balance) and fumbled around for a bit. Then he withdrew his To the Ends of the Earth & All the Realms In-Between Archaeological Compass and flipped open the lid.

"North-east," he answered, squinting at the dial in the weakened twilight.

Doris flapped her wings and lifted her claws a couple of times. "Rerk! But shouldn't we be heading to the *south*-east? That's what Fifi Glusac scribbled on that piece of pink writing paper."

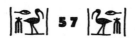

"That's true, Doris."

"Then why are we going *north*-east?"

"*Quaaaooo!*" snorted Brenda, her eyelashes bristling as she broke through the still air before her.

Jim closed the lid and slipped the compass into one of the pockets on his shirt. "We're having a small diversion. I know we've got to get down into the countryside, but I don't think that Perry would mind too much if we spent the night at an ancient site just out of Mexico City. As our plane didn't touch down till sunset, I figured we wouldn't have got very far tonight on our journey to the south-east. Now, by making a tiny detour to the north-east, we can see something truly spectacular. And then we can make an early start in the morning."

The Wonder Camel tossed her head and gave a grin. *Now* she knew why they were going in this direction.

Doris blinked impatiently. "So where exactly are we heading?" she flapped.

"Teotihuacán," Jim smiled. "The first place where Pyrella Frith photographed the Quetzal Queen!"

"Rerk."

"We might not get another opportunity to see her. The Quetzal Queen, not Miss Frith. And one thing I've learned in my career as an archaeologist: opportunities are there to be seized."

Doris gave a muffled prerking sound and felt strangely warm inside as Brenda hurtled onwards.

★ ★ ★

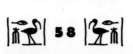

That night, as time pulled them towards the ancient site of Teotihuacán, a full moon rose above the dusty fields and straggly eucalyptus trees. Its beams were so bright that Brenda cast a dark shadow against the side of the dirt road, and Cairo Jim even thought about putting on his special desert sun-spectacles, which he had taken off when the sun had set.

At around about half-past nine Jim brought Brenda to a slower pace, and reined her off the road and onto a narrower track. There he directed her to mount a mound of dirt at the side of the track.

"Here we are, my friends," he said eagerly. "The ancient site of one of the greatest cities Mexico ever saw – Teotihuacán."

From their vantage point at the top of the mound they could see the enormous site, bathed in the strong moonbeams, spread out before them.

"Coming here at night's a good idea, you know; the last time I was here during the daytime this place was swarming with tourists and archaeologists and a convention of vacuum-cleaner sellers. Look," Jim whispered. "See that long flat avenue? That's called the Avenue of the Dead. All of those squat foundations with the sloping sides were once palaces and temples and pyramids. We think that at one stage there were *fifteen* pyramids surrounding this whole area."

"Quaaaooo," Brenda snorted, thinking how beautiful it all looked in the tranquil glow.

"And over there" – Jim pointed in another direction

– "is the Temple of the Plumed Serpent." He took his binoculars from Brenda's saddlebag and peered through them. "Look, Doris, you can just make out the heads in the moonlight."

He handed the binoculars to the macaw and she raised them to her eyes. "Rerk! For squawking out loud…"

There in the distance a small staircase rose up into the evening's gloom. On each side of this staircase, a series of carved heads was jutting out. More carved heads stuck out of the walls of the Temple, stretching out into the world as though they were trying to escape from the confines of the rock in which they were set.

Doris fluttered down onto the top of Brenda's mane, in between her ears, and held the binoculars in front of the Wonder Camel's eyes.

"Quaaaooo!"

The heads were unlike anything either Doris or Brenda had ever seen before. The faces were those of huge serpents: big, scroll-like eyes, widely flaring nostril-holes and mouths that were gaping open in chasm-like smiles, with their lips curled up at the back. Each of these mouths was filled with a conglomeration of long, curved, sharp-looking fangs. At the points where the lips curled up, at the back of each of the heads, the sculptures changed from snake to bird: big, thick carved feathers radiated out and around the heads, almost like petals around flowers.

The heads were at once fierce and beautiful.

It was several minutes before Jim spoke. "The ancient Teotihuacános called their plumed serpent *Quetzalcóatl*."

"Quetzalcóatl?" Doris squawked.

"Quetzal for the bird part," explained Jim, "cóatl for the snake part."

Doris shuddered. "I'm certainly glad there're no scales lurking about underneath *my* feathers, I can tell you. Yergh!"

Two gigantic shadows filled the binoculars' eyepieces, and Brenda snorted loudly.

"Ah, yes, my lovely," soothed Jim, patting the side of her neck. "I almost did the same thing when I first saw them too."

"Rark, did what? Saw what?" Doris pulled the binoculars back up and squinted through them. "Bleaaarrrk! They're bigger than ... bigger than ... altogether bigger than ... BIG!"

Jim laughed.

The darkness surrounded the two gigantic pyramids and seemed to make them more hulking, more dense, more sky-touching, than anything else Doris had seen in a long, long while. At the same time the moonlight cascaded down onto them and gave them a sense of being light, almost as light as air, almost as if they were hovering silently a little bit above the ground.

"When the Aztecs invaded Teotihuacán, they called that long avenue the Avenue of the Dead because they thought those beautiful pyramids were tombs that'd been built by giants for the dead rulers of this place. That pyramid at the northern end of the Avenue is called the Pyramid of the Moon. It dates to about 300 AD."

Doris gasped.

"But *that* one, the bigger one, is the Pyramid of the Sun. It's the third largest pyramid in the world, after Cholula – elsewhere in Mexico – and Khufu, back in Egypt. When more than 200,000 people lived here at Teotihuacán, the Pyramid of the Sun was painted bright red. It must have dazzled everyone in the midday sun."

"It's pretty dazzling here in the night-time dark," Doris cooed. She lifted her beak and quoted. "They 'appear as huge as high Olympus'! Rark, *Julius Caesar*, by Mr Shakespeare, Act Four, Scene Three."

"Very good, Doris."

"Thank you."

"And it's on top of the Pyramid of the Sun, on the flattish bit up there, that we're going to have our first glimpse of the Quetzal Queen!"

"Gee, Jim, those stairs look steep."

"That's because they *are*," said Jim. "The risers are steep and the treads are narrow. Why, the last time I climbed this pyramid I remember I could only fit half of my boot onto a step. The ancient people had smaller feet than we did." He gave a big sigh, full of anticipation. "You haven't lived until you've climbed the stairs of the Mexican pyramids."

"I think I'll fly up," Doris decided. "With my short legs it'd take me three weeks to climb them."

"Brenda and I'll do the climbing, won't we, my lovely?"

Brenda began to break out in a cold sweat. "How high is it, Jim?" she implored in her telepathic manner.

"Let me tell you how high it is," Jim whispered. "It's roughly the same as a nineteen-storey building – about seventy metres!"

Brenda's knees began to tremble.

Cairo Jim reined her around in the direction of the Pyramid of the Sun. "Don't you worry, Brenda, my lovely, everything'll be all right. I'll see to that."

He gave a firm yet gentle nudge with his Sahara boot and brought her down from off the mound. With Doris perched in a commanding position on the saddle's pommel, they all moved through the moonlit darkness and into the grounds of the archaeological site.

Everywhere around them was still and silent, with only the faintest breeze stirring the fine hairs on Cairo Jim's legs. The night was so serene that Doris could hear her heart *brrp brrp*ing under her feathers.

With each hoofstep she took, Brenda's dread grew. Gradually the huge, dark, looming hulk with the roughly sloping sides – the Pyramid of the Sun itself – was swelling larger and larger before her long-lashed eyes, and she started to tingle in both humps – a thing she did not enjoy at all.

"Whoa there, my lovely," Jim said quietly when they were close to the bottom of the Pyramid's staircase.

As Doris and Brenda looked up at the mighty structure, Jim reached down into his knapsack and had a bit of a delve inside. After a few moments he brought out their three torches. He gave Doris hers and, reaching forward, carefully placed Brenda's into her slightly opened jaws.

Then, as one, Jim slid his finger to the power button on his torch, Doris rustled her feathertips on her torch's button and Brenda curled her dexterous tongue around hers. Three beams of strong, steady light shot up onto the stairs.

"Raark," raarked Doris. "It sure is steep."

"Quaaaooo!" agreed Brenda as she peered up at the almost perpendicular wall of steps.

"You bet your beak and snout it is," Jim said. "Don't fret though; of all the pyramids in Mexico this one's the easiest to climb. This is the only one I've come across that has terraces running around it. See, there's one … that flat area where I'm shining my light."

Brenda trembled as she tried to shine her beam up onto the top of the staircase. But no matter how she manipulated her tongue around the torch, she was unable to find the point where the stairs ended; they seemed to go on forever. They may as well have continued all the way to the moon-filled clouds.

"Well, then," Doris chirped, "what are we waiting for? Let's go find the Quetzal Queen. See you two at the top!" She put her torch into her beak and, with a few flowing flaps, lifted off Brenda's saddle and into the air.

Jim and Brenda watched her as she flew upwards to the top of the Pyramid. At first she was easy to see as the moonlight shone on her lustrous wings. The higher she flew, though, the less visible she became, and if it hadn't been for the beam shooting out from her torch, Jim and Brenda would have had no idea of her whereabouts as the darkness engulfed her.

Then the torchlight changed direction and made a small descent until it shone out steadily from a point far above them. It blinked on and off four times and then wobbled around for a bit across a plane of darkness.

"There," whispered Jim. "That's her usual signal. She's reached the top. Now for us."

Brenda felt the ends of her eyelashes growing heavy with sweat, a sign that she was feeling exceptionally nervous. She gave a couldn't-I-just-wait-down-here-for-both-of-you type of snort, and looked around at Jim with pleading eyebrows.

"I'm so glad you're coming up with us, my lovely," he said as he patted her on the side of the neck and dismounted, jumping onto the dirt below. "We'll doubtless need your incredible Wonder Camel powers of observation once we're up there."

"Quaaoo," Brenda snorted very quietly. There was no choice about it.

"Follow me." Jim started to climb the narrow stairs, leaning forward and gripping onto the row of steps that was eight steps higher than the row he was standing on. "Just think of it like climbing a ladder.

 **65**

And remember, whatever you do on the way up: don't look down!"

A lump the size of a tennis-ball rose in the Wonder Camel's throat as her best human friend's posterior disappeared into the gloom above her. She quickly shone her torchlight onto it, nervous that if she lost sight of this bit of Cairo Jim then the whole staircase might fall over and squash her.

Soon his shorts were nothing but two wiggling stumps of gabardine growing smaller and smaller.

Come on, Brenda, she thought to herself. *Make the move. There's nothing to be frightened of. You're a Wonder Camel, after all.*

She took a gulp, lobbing the tennis-ball of terror deep down into her belly (and being careful not to accidentally swallow the torch at the same time), and slowly reared up onto her hind legs. Then, positioning her frontal hoofs onto the row of stairs level with her snout, she slowly, gingerly, *snortlessly,* began to climb.

Her frontal hoofs glinted in the moonlight as she moved them hesitantly from step to step.

Her knees rubbed against the stones in front of her as she moved higher and higher up.

Her humps felt hollow and heavy at the same time.

Her eyelashes tingled with the thought that at any time she might lose her balance and tumble backwards, head over hoofs, down the towering slope.

Gradually, however, she climbed further and further up the staircase of the Pyramid of the Sun.

About halfway up, a strange thing happened: a thought occurred to Brenda, a thought that zinged into her Wonder Camel brain like an invisible thrill of electricity.

Why don't I climb these stairs in a zigzagging motion, across this way and then across the other way, instead of going up in a straight line?

She gave it a go. First she moved her frontal hoofs a bit to the right and then hoisted the rest of her body in that direction. Then she moved a bit further to the right, and further and yet again further, climbing in that direction until she was near the right-hand edge of the staircase. And then she changed direction and began moving upwards to the left, in a diagonal line, until she came close to the left-hand edge of the staircase. Then she changed direction again, and went back – and still upwards – the other way.

Somehow it helped her. Now, instead of feeling that she was climbing up a thin, spindly rope (as she had felt when she had climbed the stairs in a straight-upwards manner), it was as if she were taking a nice, slow stroll across a slightly steep, very pebbly field.

With every step she climbed, her fear dripped away, and the sweat that had formed on her humps and other hairy bits began to evaporate.

Something had also happened to Cairo Jim halfway up the staircase of the Pyramid of the Sun. His memory had taken hold of him and had affected him in not the best of ways.

He had remembered, just as he was about to take his one hundred and twenty-fourth step, the last time he had climbed this Pyramid, some years earlier when he had been on archaeological research in Mexico. Then, he had got exactly halfway up the stairs – if his memory had been a photographic one, he would have realised that he had reached this very step itself – and a sudden, dreadful fright had overtaken him. On that occasion, the fear had welled up and over him like a monstrous cloud of swirling dust, and all that he could think about was the incredible height he was scaling and how easy it would be for him to lose his footing and plummet to the bottom in a tangle of dents and bruises and shattered desert sun-spectacles.

And this had led him to making the mistake of looking down.

Now, tonight, as the remembrance of that awful experience came back to him, he looked down again. There was the figure of Brenda, quietly snorting and climbing her way, zigzagging in fact, slowly and methodically, up the rough stairs. And below her was a blackened void that, if it had been daylight now, he would have seen to be the ground.

Cairo Jim froze in his tracks, unable to even move an eyebrow.

Above, Doris probed the staircase with her torch. Its beam picked out Jim, who seemed to be clawing onto the steps with his long, thin fingers and his heavy Sahara boots. And what was that, Doris wondered. Was her friend *trembling*?

Oh, no, Jim thought as a fat bead of perspiration trickled down his cheek, plopping onto his shirt collar. *What a time to dart up the avenue of recollection!*

He tried to lift his left hand to the step above where it was, but it was useless: he couldn't seem to release his grip from the stones.

Behind his back he could feel something, something that he knew wasn't there at all, but to his panicked, frenzied mind it *was* there – a giant, invisible hand about to pluck him from off the staircase and hurl him down, down, all the way downwards to the hard, smashing earth.

His legs went numb.

His head went hot and cold and hot again.

His back became a waterfall of moisture, drenching his shirt instantaneously.

He wished that he had had some poetry published before this awful moment.

And then Brenda nudged him with her gentle snout.

"Quaaaooo," she implored quietly. "Don't worry, Jim of Cairo, this moment will pass. Here, hold onto my bridle and we'll ascend the rest of the way together."

Jim looked down between his legs, into her wide and Wonderful eyes and saw her beautiful eyelashes fluttering at him. All at once he knew that the terror would pass. He reached down with his shaking hand and closed his fingers around her bridle.

As Brenda led him higher, his fear vanished; his memory simply blotted it all out. In no time at all they had reached the first terrace, but Brenda didn't even bother stopping there on that flat surface. She and her archaeologist-poet friend continued the climb.

Finally, they both put their hoofs and feet onto the top step. Brenda had brought herself and Jim all the way to the top – seventy metres of narrow, steep stairs.

"Phew," breathed Jim loudly. He reached out and stroked Brenda's snout as her nostrils opened and closed, gulping in the cool air around them. "Thank you, my lovely. I don't know what I would've done…"

"Quaaoo," snorted Brenda modestly.

"Raarrk!" raarrked Doris, shining her torch impatiently into Jim's face and Brenda's snout. "I thought my feathers'd go grey before you two got up here. Come and look at this, it'll knock your boots and hoofs off!"

And away went her waddling torchlight to the rear of the pyramid.

♠♠♠♠♠ 7 ♠♠♠♠♠

MOONLIT DISCOVERY

"HERE IT IS, rerk. She's even better than in Pyrella Frith's photos, what d'you reckon?"

Doris was perched by a slab of rock that was jutting out from the uppermost surface of the pyramid. With an eager wing she shone her torchbeam into the small, cave-like area underneath the overhang.

"Quaaoo," Brenda snorted as she shone her light in there as well.

Cairo Jim directed his illumination to the same spot. "Well tie me between two boards and call me a castanet!"

There lay the Quetzal Queen in all her painted and feathered glory.

"Even in the murkiness of the moonlight," Doris whispered, "and the yellowy beams from our torches, she's still as bright as can be!"

"That she is, my dear," murmured Jim, his eyes full of the colours of this extraordinary painting.

For many minutes the trio stared in silence at the vision of the Quetzal Queen who stood against a glowing peach-coloured background. Jim and Doris had seen the painting in Pyrella Frith's photographs, but now that they were actually here in front of it,

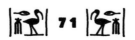

the Quetzal Queen seemed to be more than a painting; she almost seemed *alive*. Her paleness didn't seem quite as pale; her faint, amber skin was much more lifelike, and the jade-green ornaments hanging from her ears and in her nose and the light orange on her fingernails were almost bright. Her lips were a more vivid crimson, her slightly crossed eyes were of a more gleaming mauve than in the photos and her tunic was the colour of fully ripened apricots. The border patterns on the tunic seemed to spring out from the rock, so bold were they.

Jim smiled. "It's almost as if Miss Frith's photos stole away a bit of the vibrant colours, isn't it? Why, she's much gaudier here. The Quetzal Queen, I mean, not Pyrella Frith."

The most striking detail in the photos – the fountain-like headdress of shimmering green-blue quetzal feathers that rose from her hair, and flowed down the shoulders of her tunic – was here a hundred times more brilliant. The headdress seemed to leap out from the very rock itself.

"Rerk. It's as though the painting's 'newly fixed, the colour's not dry'. *The Winter's Tale*, by Mr Shakespeare, Act Five, Scene Three."

"Hmmm," pondered Jim.

Doris and Brenda shone their torches at him. They knew that when he hmmmed like that he was trying to figure something out.

"What is it, Jim?" cooed Doris.

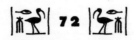

"Hmmm," he repeated, pushing back the brim of his pith helmet and scratching his forehead.

The macaw shone her torchlight to where Jim was staring. The beam came to rest on the eyes of the Quetzal Queen.

"Is it something about her eyes, Jim?"

Brenda bent her neck down and had a close inspection of the Queen's eyes. "She looks familiar," the Wonder Camel thought.

"You know," said Jim, not breaking his gaze from the painting, "those eyes look familiar somehow." He bit his lower lip and then snapped his fingers. "Of course, now I know! Brenda, my lovely, may I get something out of my knapsack, please?"

Brenda fluttered her eyelashes at him and moved closer. He reached into her saddlebag, then further into his knapsack.

"What're you looking for?" Doris prerked.

"Here it is." He pulled out the photograph that Gerald Perry Esquire had given them – the photograph of Mademoiselle Fifi Glusac.

"Just take a look at this," he said, crouching down and holding it near to the painted eyes of the Quetzal Queen.

"Quaaooo!"

"Rerk! They're identical!" Doris did a small flexing up and down routine. "The Quetzal Queen and Fifi Glusac have the same eyes!"

"That they do," frowned Cairo Jim.

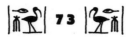

"But why," asked Doris, "would they have painted her with her eyes crossed like that?"

"Ancient vanity." Jim scratched his chin. "The ancient Mayans thought that crossed eyes were a sign of nobility and great beauty. They used to attach a small knob of chewing gum to a lock of hair that hung down between the royal babies' eyes. The babies would keep looking at this gum more than they looked at anything else. Over the years, as the babies grew, they became naturally cross-eyed."

"Ah." Doris blinked. "That explains the Quetzal Queen's peepers, then."

"No, my dear, it doesn't."

"Eh?"

"No. You see, Teotihuacán is *not* a Mayan site. The Pyramid of the Sun was built by the Toltecs, and later on invaded by the Aztecs, long before the Mayans were around. Unlike Mayan sites, there were never any human sacrifices held here. And as far as I know, the Toltecs never had a thing for crossed eyes, either." He frowned again and rubbed his bottom lip with his thumbnail. "Besides which, they would never have been able to find the chewing gum to tie to her lock of hair when she was a baby. No, that gum only comes from the trees in the jungles, in those other places where Miss Pyrella Frith took the photos."

He shone his torch on the photograph of Fifi Glusac, then at the Quetzal Queen, then back on Fifi Glusac. "Hmmm. Something's not right about all this…"

"*Quaaaooo!*"

Brenda's loud snort made Jim jump and Doris flutter a little way into the air.

"What is it, my lovely?"

The Wonder Camel gestured with her head in a wide oblong shape all around the painting of the Quetzal Queen.

"Well, I'll be gouached," Jim muttered.

"Plait my plumes," Doris squawked.

Brenda had noticed something that the others hadn't seen, something that hadn't shown up in Pyrella Frith's pictures: surrounding the painting was an intricate border of small, square shapes.

"Glyphs!" exclaimed Jim, running his torchlight over them. "Ancient Mexican glyphs!"

Some of them were of faces, some of unusual shapes, some of dots and others were made up of lines with rounded ends.

"Good one, Bren," prerked Doris.

"Quaaooo," snorted Brenda.

"Can you decipher it, Doris?" Jim asked.

"Is water wet?" asked Doris in a mock-superior manner (for, after all, ancient picture languages and archaic means of communication were her speciality).

She hop-fluttered all around the border of intricacy. "It looks like it's made up of a series of different glyphs, Jim, but the same series is repeated on all four sides of the border. See? The pattern on this side is the same as the pattern on this side over here" – she flew to the opposite side – "and that's the same as that one over there."

"The same series repeated four times," muttered Jim. "What do they say?"

"Quaaooo," said Brenda, putting in her two-snorts worth.

"Let's see. Aherm." Doris cleared her throat, shut one eye and slowly began to waddle the length of the right-hand-side border, carefully enunciating as she went:

"Monty Zoomah ha ha ha

me a genius by far

one day soon my name be known

Neptune Flannelbottom Bone!"

All around Teotihuacán, the air went still. For a brief moment, the strong beams from the full moon were broken by a shifting cloud mass, grey and billowing against the thick, dark sky.

The photograph of Fifi Glusac slipped out of Jim's fingers and fell next to the Quetzal Queen. Four slightly crossed eyes – two on the photo, two on the painting – stared up at Jim, Doris and Brenda.

"What monstrous, vile skulduggery is he up to *this* time?" whispered Cairo Jim.

♦♦♦♦♦ 8 ♦♦♦♦♦

IN JUNGLED GLOOM...

"CRARK," croaked Desdemona loudly. She was perched on the old travelling trunk in the back seat of the Bugatti automobile that Neptune Bone had rented upon their arrival in Mexico City, some days earlier.

"What's up with you, you dreadful dominion of dullness?" sneered the fleshy man as he watched the roadway ahead.

Her beak shot around to her netherfeathers and pecked off a tiny battalion of fleas. She cracked them apart in her mouth, and the tiny creatures slithered across her rough, yellow tongue, down her gullet and into her paunch. Then she eyed Bone in his rear-vision mirror. "I'm uncertain, that's what's up with me."

"Uncertain?"

"Yep. All of me is uncertain. I haven't got a clue as to why we're doing all of this, and I don't like it."

Bone steered the car around a large pot-hole on the jungle-lined road and clenched his cigar firmly between his teeth. "Perhaps you would like a little enlightenment, Desdemona?"

"No, forget about all that. I just want to know what's going on. I mean to squawk, here we are, with La Stupido in a travelling trunk—"

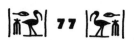

"La Stupido? Very good. Arrr."

"And we're bumping away into the middle of the jungle, to a place that – if I'm not very much mistaken – we've already been to and painted old feather-head onto the temple of. Why? Why, why, *why* have we been coming to Mexico for the last six months and painting pretty pictures on old, abandoned sites and then kidnapping Mademoiselle here and returning and upsetting my belly all the while with these confounded re-fried beans?" She stopped her moaning and clutched at her stomach. "Uh-oh, I think them fleas I just swallowed have hit the beans. Uggghhh. Now my *guts* are uncertain. I feel like I'm a volcano about to erupt from the wrong end!"

"Well don't do it on the Bugatti or I'll never get my deposit back when I return it to the hire place."

"Crark." The raven fluttered her wings over her middle, soothing herself and trying not to think about her inner turbulence. "I wish *I* could be in a *higher place* right now. Anywhere but here."

"You could just fly off, if you weren't on the Wanted List of every branch of the Antiquities Squad from here to Dodoma." His cigar smoke curled up and around his petunia-coloured fez. "Maybe I should explain a little bit more about all of this great enterprise I've masterminded, before your uncertainty rises up and causes something nasty to happen to you. Although *what* could be nastier than your natural scrofulous state, I have no idea."

"Ha, ha," she rasped, but her voice was curious.

"Flutter to me here, though, Desdemona; I don't want La Stupido to overhear at this stage."

Desdemona hopped over the seat and perched on the top of the windscreen next to the steering wheel.

"This whole elaborate scheme – which, when fully realised, will illuminate my glorious genius like no other scheme I have ever devised – came to me about three years ago. Quite suddenly. All because I tripped over."

Desdemona's eyes throbbed redly as she squinted at him.

"It was about the time that we made that very narrow escape from Inspector Mustafa Kuppa of the Maxwell House Branch of the Antiquities Squad in Hurghada. After we'd been looking for the sunken sarcophagus of Pharaoh Sekheret. As you know, after that escapade I had to get out of Kuppa's way quick-smart whenever he caught up with me."

"Hey, wait a minute, Captain! It wasn't only you. He wanted my quills as well, remember!"

"Arrr, so he did. But, for once in your miserable life, you were lucky, birdbrain. You had a quick and easy means of evading him and all his goody-goody forces. You just raised those tatty feathered wings of yours and you were gone. I must say you can be swift when the need arises."

She sniggered and pecked a flea off her wingtip.

"I, on the other hand, could not take immediate refuge in the skies. I needed a place to escape to, somewhere I could not be found or bothered, until Mustafa Kuppa had started to forget about the little

Sekheret incident. Somewhere that the rest of the world had *completely* forgotten about."

"You went to *New Zealand*?" gasped Desdemona.

"No, I did not. There were two other obvious places I could hide: the jungles of Mexico or the back streets of Port Moresby. As I owe my Port Moresby tailor a large amount of money for those tasteful floral and fleur-de-lis shirts he made for me seventeen years ago, it had to be the jungles of Mexico."

"You owe him almost as much as you owe the Old Relics Society in overdue membership fees. But I thought you hated jungles and rainforests and all that greenery?"

"I most certainly do. But I also hate the thought of being apprehended by the Antiquities Squad and going to jail. So I jumped onto a barge full of used swizzle-sticks and high-tailed it over here."

"So that's where you got to. I couldn't find you for months. When I couldn't trace you I even thought you'd become a theatrical agent."

"Perish the thought! And it was here, in the south-east of Mexico, that I stumbled and tripped. It was, you fearsome flying feruncle, to be a fall into ever-growing greatness!"

"Eh?"

"This is what happened. I had made my camp somewhere in the jungly bits in the south-east of Mexico. Where *exactly* I have never been able to recall. One night, after a tasty meal of avocados, corn frajitas and re-fried beans, and after I had manicured my lustrous fingernails to my satisfaction and had smoked several dozen Belch of Brouhaha cigars, I decided to go for a quiet and introspective stroll into the undergrowth."

"You mean, you needed to do a—"

"*I mean I needed to take a quiet and introspective stroll in the undergrowth!* Sometimes geniuses such as what I am have to take our subtle grandeur and be alone with it, away from the lesser life forms. So I got a lighted branch from my camp-fire and a roll of lavatory paper – er, to write down any sudden bursts of brilliance I might have had while on my walk—"

"That's one way of putting it!"

"Shut your beak. And off I went. Now, I hadn't walked for more than five minutes when suddenly I fell face-down into a thick cluster of fallen leaves. Big leaves, huge things that had come down from the canopy of the rainforest, far above. Normally jungles and rainforests conspire against me, but this time I was lucky: because the leaves were so thick and springy, I did not bruise my face or chip any fingernails in my fall.

"I rolled over and smoothed down my waistcoat, checking that my gold fob-watch had not been dented or shattered, and then I realised something. I had not tripped over the *pile of leaves*, but over a low line of stones that lay in front of it."

"Stones?"

"Stones that had been placed side-by-side to form a small ridge, somewhat like a very squat wall, and which didn't even come halfway up to the hem of my plus-fours trousers.

"I grabbed up my lighted branch and began to inspect this bit of masonry. Although crudely constructed, it had clearly been made by human beings because of the way the stones had been laid in an overlapping manner.

"Being an ever-inquiring sort of genius, I carefully started to clear the moss and lichens from the stones. I thought that maybe the stones might have been ancient gold blocks or something equally as fabbo-doodie!"

"Were they? Were they fabbo-doodie gold?"

"Arrr, they were fabbo-doodie, all right." Bone quickly ashed his cigar into the wind, aiming the ashes so that they would blow back into Desdemona's beak, which they did.

"Blecchhh!" She shook her head and flicked the ashes from her eyes. "Gold, gold, you found gold! That's much better than rubies! Oh, you clever big—"

"They *weren't* gold, you excitable effluence."

"Eh? Ratso."

"They contained something far more valuable than gold or rubies or any sort of preciousness that human beings recognise."

"What? What did they contain?"

"Glyphs," answered Bone, his eyes flashing like two small fires, as the car bumped along.

"Glyphs?"

"Arrrr."

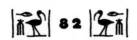

"You mean, just ancient carvings from some forgotten language?"

"I most certainly do."

"And what," she spat mockingly, "is so precious about a whole lot of moss-covered glyphs?"

"The story they had to tell me," whispered Neptune Bone.

"Story?" sneered Desdemona. "What sort of story?"

"The best sort of story. A totally *forgotten* one! Arrr." His flabby lips curled around his cigar in a caress of satisfaction. "A story that took place many, many years ago in these parts. One that will take place again, and more importantly, *one that will take place for ever and a day*!"

"Tell me, tell me, tell me!"

"You might prepare yourself for what I discovered on that fateful evening with a bit of respectful patience, you atrociously attired aberration. It was indeed a monumental find. You see, as I cleared away the moss and other obscuring fungi, the glyphs told me the tale of a Mayan Queen, a queen who had reigned in these particular parts for a great period of time."

"The Quetzal Queen?" asked Desdemona.

"The Quetzal Queen herself. At first, when I read in the glyphs that she had been ruler for many rains and many sun-blazing scorching seasons, I was unimpressed. There have, after all, been oodles of sovereigns in oodles of countries in the last millennium who have reigned for decades and decades. But slowly, as I uncovered more of the story, I started to realise that it wasn't just *decades* that this Queen had ruled for. At last I pulled away an especially large bit of jungle-goo that was covering a particularly elaborate carved set of glyphs, and every pore in my great and brilliant hide tingled with the sort of exhilaration that you get when you have found something that has been discarded into the dusty vaults of time!"

"Yes? Yes, yes, yes? What'd the glyphs say?"

"They told me that the Quetzal Queen had ruled over all of her peoples for no less than seven hundred and eighty-nine years!"

"Craaarrrk!"

"Think of it, Desdemona! A single human being, reigning for all that time. I sat down on the leaves, dazed and confused. Yes, I admit it, I was *confused*, a thing that has only happened to me once before in my lifetime, and that was at my moment of birth. How could such a thing be *possible*?"

"That's easy – your mother and your father must've got all lovey-dovey and—"

"No, boffinbeak, not my *birth*, I mean how could the Quetzal Queen have reigned for so long? I pondered this for many minutes and then I turned back to the glyphs for the answer.

"The low wall of stones continued into the undergrowth, which gradually got thicker and thicker. I worked hard that night, clearing and scraping, and recording everything on the lavatory paper I had brought along with me. Thank heavens for modern comforts when one has to self-exile oneself into the remotest places! By the time the sun had deigned to show itself, I had come to what looked like the end of the wall of stones.

"Finally, on the very last three stones in the wall, I found the answer: the Quetzal Queen was able to reign for such a colossal amount of time not because she was a god, but because of something rare and extremely valuable. Something that was made by her tribe of people, just for her. Something that made her life *very* livable."

"What, what was it? Special orthopaedic sandals with little nobbly things on the innersoles that helped her keep her posture? False teeth made of jewels? Artificial hip replacements? Ancient daytime television?"

"No, stupid, something far greater. A unique elixir!"

"A unique *what*-er?"

"A tonic, a concoction, a glorious goluption of a potion which she drank every morning and evening for the entire procession of her life. According to the glyphs in the jungle, it was known as the Elixir of Eternity!"

Desdemona gasped, and stared out into the roadway ahead. The day was wearing on into late afternoon. Soon the sun would be setting and already, because of the thick greenery that bordered the road, long, dark shadows were spreading across the car's pathway. Neptune Bone reached down and with a small grunt turned on the Bugatti's headlights.

"This Elixir of Eternity meant that the Quetzal Queen would never, *ever* grow old. She would remain youthful forever and ever, and would shine as long as the sun and moon. Never would she see old age!"

"Nevermore, nevermore, nevermore," crarked the raven.

"There the stones – and these all-revealing glyphs of my salvation – ran out. I carefully made sure I had transcribed all of this breathtaking rampage of knowledge onto my lavatory paper and the next day I promptly vamoosed out of the jungle and went straight up to the Mexico City Library. There, cunningly disguised as Dame Nellie Melba – just in case there were any Antiquities Squad Members still sniffing after me, you understand – I spent many hours perusing all the history books relating to the south-east of Mexico. Here is where my only obstacle accosted me." He gave a contemptuous snort through his wide nose.

"Oh, yeah? What was that? Was your frock too tight? Did your corset pinch? Was your over-the-shoulder boulder hol—"

"Enshut your beak, you disgraceful excuse for a collection of chromosomes! No, it had nothing to do with my disguise. It was very comfortable, if you want to know, especially the soft lacy bits I … oh, why do I *bother*? No, the problem was that in my eager haste to leave the jungles and come to the library in Mexico

City, I had neglected to make an exact note of where I had been camped, and consequently where I had stumbled across the glorious glyphs. And I had no idea where I was when I had set up camp in the jungle; I had hurried to find the most remote patch of isolated bushy bits that I could, and so hadn't bothered to consult my compass.

"Well, to cut a fat story slender, I made some very interesting discoveries in the library in Mexico City. Do you know, Desdemona, that there are certain historians who believe that the Mayan descendants of the Quetzal Queen herself are still living in the jungles down here?"

Desdemona slapped a wing across her eyes. "I get it, I get it, I get it," she crowed. "And these descendants still have the recipe for this Elixir, yes?"

"Arrr. So the books say. That is why we have been coming back and forth to Mexico."

She shot her beak around to face him. "Now, hang on just a momento. I still don't get it. How come you spent so much time painting those ridiculous paintings? And why did you do them in so many different places? Teotihuacán, Palenque—"

"Which is where we're headed now, oh squawking squab of squalor."

"—Chichén Itzá, Uxmal ... why did you do all of *that*?"

"The reasons are simple. Firstly I painted all of those wonderful portraits because, according to all the books I consulted, there has never been found a likeness of the actual Quetzal Queen. Nobody knows what she looked like. Isn't that fortuitous for us?"

"Um … I guess so," muttered Desdemona, who didn't really know what "fortuitous" meant.

"And secondly, I painted the portraits in all of those locations because as I told you before, I can't exactly recollect where I had made the discovery of the glyphs that told me of the Queen's incredible longevity. The first painting I did, on the top of the Pyramid of the Sun at Teotihuacán, was only a test-run; the pyramid was close to Mexico City, where we had swiped all those over-priced paints and brushes from that art-supply shop, and so it seemed a good place to have a bit of a practice at the finer arts involved in the re-creation of history. It wasn't a bad painting, if I do say so myself, although it was, to my refined eye, a little too *bright*. But the others I painted … now, *they* were astonishingly excellent!"

"It's all still as clear as mud. Why paint them in the first place?"

"To entice the natives out, thistlehead. To lure them into my sphere of influence, with their Elixir of Eternity."

The raven looked as baffled as a dish-mop.

"And because I am not exactly sure *where* this particular tribe of the Quetzal Queen's descendants lives, I had to paint those different images of her at the three most important locations in the south-east of Mexico, roughly in the broad area where I was camped, in order to bring the natives forth. Hopefully, one out of the three ancient sites will be close to the Queen's tribe. And, even *more* hopefully, our visit may entice the tribe out from its jungly hideaway."

"How can you be so sure?"

"I read it, you doubting dumdum. One of those dusty books in Mexico City Library told me that according to the legend the tribe will show itself on the night the Queen returns. It's a good thing that the tribe will only come out at night, in my esteemed opinion; by day, these sites are always overcrowded with tourists and archaeologists and vacuum-cleaner sellers attending nearby conventions."

Suddenly the Bugatti hit an unseen pot-hole, and the front tyres shot into the air.

"*Scraarrk!*" screamed Desdemona, momentarily flung upwards and off the car.

Bone gripped the steering wheel tightly, his knuckles bulging against his fine driving gloves. He whizzed the wheel around and around, and the front tyres hit the dirt again. Desdemona fluttered down onto the top of the windscreen.

"That was close," growled Bone.

"'Ey!" came the muffled protest from Fifi Glusac, together with some hard rappings on the inside of the trunk. "Watch it, you stupid man. I'm getting bruises on my bruises in 'ere!"

"Oh, we don't want *that*, Mademoiselle," Bone called over his flabby shoulder. He lowered his voice and spoke to the bird. "No, I don't imagine the Indians will want to hand over their Elixir to a *bruised* Quetzal Queen, do you, Desdemona?"

At this point the peso finally dropped for the raven. "Oh, my goodness gracious," she gasped. "You mean *you*—?"

"How else do you think I shall be able to live and breathe and *rule* forevermore? *AAAAAAAAR-RRRRRRRRRR!*"

Part Two:

THE INJURING OF ETERNITY?

9

PERSUASION AT PALENQUE

THE MOON THAT NIGHT spilled down onto the Mexican landscape, casting a shimmering blanket of light over the mountains and the rocky coastal outcrops, bathing the small villages and the dark, sleeping jungles in its gentle glow.

In the centre of this vast land the moonbeams glinted off a small trio as it moved steadily eastwards. The roads were rough in many places and tough underhoof, but Brenda the Wonder Camel was not disturbed by this, for she was being drawn, like a magnet, towards the jungled ruins of Palenque.

Perched with worried feathers on Brenda's rear hump, Doris scanned the night ahead with alert eyes. She rode silently as she puzzled over what Neptune Bone was up to.

Sitting erect and earnest in Brenda's saddle, Jim of Cairo rode silently also. He had decided to set out directly from Teotihuacán after they had found the Quetzal Queen with Bone's rude glyphs on top of the Pyramid of the Sun, even though it had still been deep night. So Brenda had started on the long trek, almost a full day behind the Bugatti of Bone.

As the Wonder Camel's mighty hoofs pounded along the roadway, the rhythm of her movement seeped into

Jim's spine, travelling quickly upwards into the back of his neck. Then it spread out, like a runny egg in a frying pan, into the archaeologist's poetry cells, and the new rhythm pounded through his brain:

> *The world may be a huge canvas*
> *with stories painted near and far*
> *that hold the key to ancient tales*
> *as old as space's first-formed star;*
> *and while some of these tales are good*
> *and should be told and told again,*
> *others will be clutched and used*
> *by arrogant and evil men.*

Cairo Jim pushed the brim of his pith helmet up from his forehead and wiped the sweat from his brow with the back of his hand. Palenque was still a long way ahead.

With a sleek purring, the Bugatti turned off the highway and onto the short track that led to the jungle-threaded ruins of Palenque. Neptune Bone knew the area well enough – he had taken his time when he was last here, lingering inside the temple at the top of the many-staired Tomb of Pakal, until he had got the Quetzal Queen looking just the way he wanted.

The car glided to the end of the track and Bone turned off the engine. He threw open the small door and squeezed his bulky bottom off the seat and through the doorway. Then, standing next to the vehicle, he stretched his arms towards the stars.

"Arrrrr," he moaned with a mixture of pleasure (at being able to stretch his limbs) and anticipation (at the thought of his neverending, rich life), and cracked his knuckles loudly.

"ARRRRRK," cried Desdemona, flapping about on the hood. "I wish you wouldn't do that. It makes my stomach go gooier than it already is."

"You delicate dregbucket of drivel," sneered Bone. He took a Belch of Brouhaha cigar from inside his emerald-green waistcoat and lit it with his silver cigar-lighter. With a strong exhalation, he blew the first shaft of foul-smelling smoke straight into the raven's throbbing eyeballs.

"Hergh," she spluttered. "Thanks a lot. That *really* helps. Ooooh…" Her wingtips massaged her pot belly. "I think I'm going to—" She clamped one wing across her beak and the other over her other end.

"Then fly, Desdemona. Go on, into the trees. I don't want your reeking eruptions anywhere in my vicinity."

She gave him a filthy look – for a brief moment she thought how nice his fez would be decorated with her inner turbulence – and then flapped up and off to the nearest cluster of vine-tangled trees.

Bone watched her disappear against the moon. When she was out of sight, he reached into the car and took out a small crowbar from under the driver's seat. Then, being very careful not to damage any of his precious fingernails (even though he was still wearing his driving gloves), he prised open the lock of the lacklustre travelling trunk.

The lid lurched open and out onto the back seat spilled Fifi Glusac, her arms and legs twisted around each other in such a complicated way that she looked like a small bundle of frozen white snakes.

"Arr," smiled Bone. "So nice of you to join me."

Fifi looked up at him as he straddled the night, gloating in the moonlight. Very carefully she started to unravel her tangle, bit by bit, taking her left arm from behind her neck and her right leg out of the crook between her other leg and her nose.

When she had found all of her toes again she stood slowly and had a tiny, but oft-rehearsed, wriggle. Then she stepped from the car and drew herself down to Bone's full height.

"Now, you listen to moi, m'sieur!" she snarled. "You 'ave broken ze laws as I know zem. You 'ave no right to kidnap an artiste of my calibre and bring moi all ze way to Mexico! If I weren't such a lady I would 'ave you on ze ground, rolling around in agony, before you would know what 'ad 'appened. But I shall not stoop to such brutish be'aviour. No, I shall 'ave you arrested and 'urled into ze lock-up! Zen you will wish zat you 'ad never barged into my dressing room in ze first place!"

Bone blew smoke into her messed-up blonde curls. "I think not, mademoiselle," he leered.

"I zink so!"

"No, I think not. I think that you will, in fact, help me in my little quest."

"Ooh, you are so ... so smug! You zink you know what I will do? 'Oo do you zink you are?"

Bone clamped the cigar in his teeth and slowly pulled off his driving gloves, finger socket by finger socket, before he answered her. "I am merely a genius, mademoiselle. The top of my field, just as you are." He puffed smoke casually as he rubbed the fingernails on his left hand with the fleshy underneath bit of his right-hand pinkie finger. "And it is precisely because I *am* a genius that I can read you like a road map."

Fifi Glusac snarled quietly and clutched her fists by her sides. But she said nothing.

"I weigh things up," Bone continued in a superior tone. "The facts. The reality of your current situation. And out of all of it, I conclude that which is obvious: firstly, you may *want* to have me arrested, but you can't. Not right at the moment, at least. There isn't a gendarme for miles around, and even if you opened that slender throat of yours and hollered for one, it would be to no avail – we are quite isolated out here in the jungles. The only thing you might attract if you started screaming would be a brigade of curious armadillos, and they don't have much sway with the forces of justice, I'm here to tell you."

Fifi's eyes flashed at his illumination of the truth.

"Secondly, you are an entertainer, a purveyor and constructor of *the pretend*. You and your lot are known to make the most out of any grim situation ... you have a thing which you fall back upon, a wretched quality they call *optimism*. You pretend that things are not as bad as they seem. So I deduce that you will realise that there is no use to keep working *against* me while we are stuck here in Mexico's desolate extremities, and you will, for the time being at least, decide to work *with* me. You will choose to make the most of your predicament, and keep a twinkle in your eyes and a spring in your step – to quote some boringly popular tunes I had the misfortune to hear on the wireless."

"Mph! You're wrong, buster!"

"I am never wrong. You will decide to assist me in the getting of my treasure."

"Never in a zillion years."

"And do you want to know *why* you will want to assist me?"

Fifi remained silent, but raised her chin and looked at him with a fleck of curiosity in the corners of her eyes.

"I'll tell you," Bone smiled, ashing the cigar onto the ground. "You will want to assist me because I can give you something you would greatly love to own."

"Oh, oui?" Her voice was low, but not as harsh as before.

"Oui." Now his voice was changing also, becoming more conversation-like and less proclaiming. He raised an eyebrow in a hairy gesture of friendship. "You see, La Stupi ... er, La Stupenda, I have read about you in many of those theatrical magazines that cover the news-stands like unimaginative birds stuck to a power pole. You know the magazines I mean: *Writhing in the Wings, Variety, This Week in Greasepaint, Contortionists' Monthly, Bend and Stretch, Tangling Without Dangling.* And I've discovered a few very interesting things about your personal life…"

"Such as? Go on, M'sieur Zoomah."

"Such as the fact that, when you are not busy tangling yourself up and blowing into that poor excuse for a miniature brass band, you like nothing better than to stay at home in your apartment and have a good fiddle with your extensive feather collection."

"Ah!" Fifi gasped. "You *do* know about moi!"

"I can almost remember the exact words from the article that I read: 'Mademoiselle Fifi Glusac, arguably the world's best simultaneous contortionist and harmonica player, certainly leads a busy – if complicated – life. When she's not enthusiastically playing the classics and getting herself into positions that most ordinary people would only ever contemplate if there was no alternative, she has a special way of relaxing: she pulls down the blinds and spends hours alone with her feather collection, privately cataloguing her vast array of quills from all around the globe. And to think that *this* is what tickles her fancy!' Arrrr."

"Oui," shuddered Fifi. "I remember zat story. Ze reporter was very inquisitive."

"He certainly was. Arrr." Bone reached into the Bugatti and rummaged around on the floor. Fifi watched as his massive, chequered-covered bottom moved this way and that as he searched. Then he straightened himself and held aloft a long stick, on the end of which was a carefully bound bundle of rags and twine. It looked like Bone was holding a giant matchstick. "I read the rest of what that reporter wrote, and quickly came to learn that there is one type of feather you do *not* possess in your comprehensive collection."

"You mean—?"

"Yes, mademoiselle, the pitch-black feather of the species known as the rare Flitty Egyptian Raven."

"Oh, I 'ave been after such a specimen for years and years. Zey are so 'ard to obtain."

"That is where I can help you. But I can do better than just *one* feather from the rare Flitty Egyptian Raven." He wiggled his eyebrows in what he imagined was an enticing manner. "If you go along with my plan while we're here in Mexico, I can guarantee you a whole *sackful* of the feathers!" He took his cigar-lighter from the pocket of his waistcoat and opened the cover.

"You mean...?"

"Yes, La Stupenda, the bird you know as petite Dessie is, by pure chance, a rare Flitty Egyptian Raven. You could have no finer feathers than hers; she comes from a noble pedigree. Her great-great-grandmother was none other than the very raven who swooped into the library of the poet Edgar Allan Poe, once upon a midnight dreary, while he pondered weak and weary, many years ago."

"You don't say?" Fifi's eyes were ablaze with a collector's passion.

"And petite Dessie has inherited much of her great-great-grandmother's gloomy nature. Although not when it comes to her feathers. Oh, no. I know they look a tad drab and flea-infested right now, but, Mademoiselle, when they have all been plucked off and turbo-cleaned, they will be the crowning plumes of your collection! People will pay great homage to you. You will find new areas of respect from the public!"

"Respect? I don't get a lot of *zat* for what I do." She tossed back her tangled curls and fixed him with a hard stare. "All right, m'sieur. I *will* 'elp you. But only until you get your rubies."

"Let us call them *my invaluable treasure*, shall we?"

"And zen, when you 'ave got your 'ands on *your invaluable treasure*, *I* shall get *my* 'ands on *my* invaluable treasure and I shall never see you again."

"A perfect agreement. Arrr." He flicked the flint of the cigar-lighter and a long flame danced up into the night. This he put to the bundle at the top of the stick, and it ignited with an undelayed *whoosh*. "I'm just lighting this to let the natives know we're here. It is they who will hopefully lead us to our invaluable treasures this very night."

There was a violent flapping in the air above, and the heavy swishing of branches. Bone froze, his eyes wide and frigid, his breathing almost slowing down to nothing.

"M'sieur Zoomah, what is ze matter? You look like you 'ave—"

"Shhh!" he hissed. He peered up through his thick eyebrows into the darkness. "That sound…"

"Why, you are sweating like a minor waterfall!"

"*Shhh!*"

But he said no more, for at that moment Desdemona descended from the dimness and came to rest on the front left-hand mudguard of the car. "Crarrrk, that's better. I feel like I've been lightened of a great and heavy burden."

"Arrr, it's only you," breathed Neptune Bone with relief.

"Who'dja think it was?" Desdemona eyed him suspiciously. "Shirley Temple?"

"My nemesis," shuddered the fleshy man. He held the lighted torch away from his face and dabbed at his sweat-studded brow with his handkerchief.

"Oh, yes," crowed the raven. "From Samothraki."*

Bone shot her a shut-your-beak glare.

"Bonjour, you beautiful specimen of feathery fancy."

Desdemona glared at Fifi, then at Bone, then at Fifi

---

* See *Cairo Jim and the Alabastron of Forgotten Gods: A Tale of Disposable Despicableness.*

again. "What's with the tangler?" she whispered out of the side of her beak to Bone.

"She has," he sneered, adjusting his fez and regaining his boldness, "decided to see the light." He held the blazing torch above his fez and waved it slowly through the air. "No pun intended, of course. Arrrrr."

"Ha-crark-har," spat the raven.

All around them, the jungle was enveloped by a soft, but steady, symphony: croakings and chatterings and whistlings and screechings; branches rustling and palm-fronds sighing. Every now and then, a sharp cracking would be heard, as a bough from some tree that was as ancient as the ruins it watched over snapped from its trunk and flumped to the thickly padded mulch of the forest floor.

Fifi Glusac gasped. "M'sieur Zoomah, look! Zere, be'ind ze trees! Coming around zat huge staircase!"

"What?" croaked Desdemona, peering into the darkness. "What is it?"

"Yes, mademoiselle," Bone whispered. "I see it. There, Dessie, look, over by the far boundary of the Temple of Inscriptions and the Tomb of Pakal."

They all watched silently, sucking their breaths in, as a faint, glowing light flickered and danced through the night-blue forest.

"Well I'll be a raving raven!"

"And," purred Neptune Bone, "as sure as I'm a genius, it appears to be coming this way!" He quickly plunged the top part of himself into the Bugatti and, after a swift rummage, straightened again, clutching a huge headdress of bright green-blue nylon feathers and an assortment of plastic, jade-green, clip-on jewellery in his pudgy hand.

"Hurry, madam, plonk this onto your head and these in your nose and on your ears, before the seconds conspire against us all!"

10

IN THE WAKE OF A GENIUS

ANOTHER DAY HAD PASSED in the jungles. Another sun had risen, and the forest life had spent the daylight hours going about its business. Toucans had screeched and gathered and nested; snakes had coiled around tree branches and burrowed down underneath enormous, loosely packed mattresses of leaves and bark, to find the cool of the bottom of the forest; iguanas had basked on carefully chosen ledges of rock that were exposed to the warming sunlight.

And, at the large ruins of Palenque, where the mighty Mayan king Pakal had reigned nearly a millennium and a half ago, the busloads of tourists had visited. *Their* chatter and basking and burrowing had rivalled all of the native inhabitants' everyday routine.

Now the daylight hours were drawing to a slow close. The animals and birds and reptiles were settling down to their noisy pre-night-time rituals. The tourists had left, their buses and small vans driving off into the last rays of day.

The ruins of Palenque were still and regal, like silent giants sitting wearily and alone in the jungle-surrounded clearings. The many crumbling window hollows in the hilltop Temple of the Doves and the

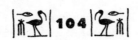

Royal Palace seemed to look out across the evening like scores of half-opened eyes.

And there, in the midst of all the stillness, a small party had arrived.

"Whoa, my lovely!" cried Cairo Jim, bringing Brenda to a slow halt before the Tomb of Pakal.

"Quaaaooo," snorted the nearly exhausted Wonder Camel. She rolled her huge head, and enormous drops of sweat flew off in all directions.

"Good ride, Bren," squawked Doris, fluttering her wingtips over Brenda's fore hump. "I'm going to have a quick reconnoitre, okay, Jim?"

"Good idea, my dear."

"Rark," screeched Doris. She flapped quietly off into the air.

Jim jumped down from Brenda's saddle and, without hesitation, fished out her deep water-bowl from one of the saddle-pockets. This he set on the ground in front of the gasping beast. Then he took out a large bottle of water and filled the bowl to the brim.

"Quaaaooo," she snorted, fluttering her eyelashes appreciatively. Jim smiled, and Brenda pushed her snout into the bowl.

Cairo Jim stretched his limbs while Brenda slurped away. He grabbed his binoculars and peered around the site, at the ancient buildings all about. The light was growing weaker by the minute, and a drifting vapour of thin mist was beginning to gather.

His magnified gaze passed across the stone walls of

the Palace, stretching away towards the thick, dense trees at the eastern end of the site. There appeared to be no sign of life or movement by the walls. Jim looked further up, at the Palace's tower. The windows stared vacantly down at him.

"Hmm," Jim pondered to Brenda. "There are lots of passageways and corridors in the Palace, perfect places for somebody to be hiding, but I don't think we'll find Bone in there. For one thing, it'll be a lot dimmer inside there than it is out here, and if he *was* inside he'd have lit a fire or have a lamp burning by now. And we'd be able to see that."

Brenda lifted her head and licked her lips as she listened.

Next, Jim turned and moved the binoculars past the darkened trees, towards the Temple of the Inscriptions. Slowly he looked up the sixty-nine steep steps until he came to view the temple on top, with its walls of carefully carved reliefs of long-dead Mayan nobles.

"See up there, my lovely? That's where Miss Frith found the second painting of the Quetzal Queen. The second example of Bone's dreadful handiwork. Deep down inside the Temple you can find the tomb of Pakal himself."

"Quaaooo."

"And look!" He adjusted the focus on the binoculars. "There's Doris, beckoning us with her wing. Come on, let's get up those stairs."

Brenda fluttered her eyelashes eagerly; she was

actually looking forward to another steep climb, after having found her new skills at Teotihuacán.

"Come on, come on," Doris muttered to herself as she waddled along the top step of the Temple of the Inscriptions. "Hurry up!" She squinted into the gloom as she watched the archaeologist-poet and the Wonder Camel move slowly up the staircase of narrow ledges.

Jim breathed carefully and steadily as he ascended. This time he did not let himself think about what he was doing, or how high he was climbing. Instead, he turned his mind to poetry, and he slowly breathed out his new verses in between steps:

> The other day upon the stair
> I met a lonely eyebrow hair.
> It filled me with a little sorrow –
> hair today, but gone tomorrow?

And,

> Let us go to Mexico,
> Let us find for Perry
> something rare, mysterious,
> something legendary...

These simple rhymes helped distract him from his fear of climbing.

Brenda came forth, zigzagging confidently to the left and to the right, her mane bristling with

accomplishment while she still kept a watchful eye on Jim of Cairo.

After what seemed like a decade to Doris, Jim and Brenda were at the top. Jim pushed his pith helmet back from his brow and sat on the uppermost step, puffing loudly.

"Rark! It's about time. You took so long I thought my feathers were about to grow feathers of their own!"

Jim leaned over and gave her crest a gentle tousle. "You eager bird, you," he smiled.

Doris blinked, and the plumes around the side of her beak blushed. She shook her head quickly to get rid of her embarrassment.

"Any sign of Bone?" Jim asked, leaning across to Brenda (who was sitting close by) and taking out from her saddlebag all three of their torches. He handed these to his friends.

"Come and see what's happened, and you'll both see *why* I'm so eager!" Doris fluttered off into the Temple.

Carefully, Brenda clip-clopped off after her. Jim stood and followed as well.

They switched on their torches and shone them around the room. Along the back wall, a clear series of Mayan glyphs was carved on three panels. Doris had a quick scan of them.

"See?" she prerked. "It says the Temple was dedicated in 692 AD, and that it's known as the Temple of Inscriptions. Plus it says a whole lot of other things, too. But that's not why I'm eager."

She hopped across the floor. "Shine your lights down here," she commanded.

Jim and Brenda did so.

"It's the work of fat feet, all right," Doris squawked.

The painting of the Quetzal Queen lay before them, but now, rather than being clear and defined as it had been when they had seen it in Pyrella Frith's photos, it was horribly scuffed and scratched. It was as though the colours on the deep green background had been smashed apart: her faint amber skin, her jade-green ornaments that had been in her ears and nose, the light orange of her fingernails and the crimson of her lips had all been blasted every which way. Her slightly crossed eyes were now completely obliterated, and the shimmering green-blue feathered headdress was nothing more than a wild smudge at the top of the ruined border.

"If this were a *genuine* painting from the ancient days," muttered Jim, "I'd be beside myself with rage. Thank goodness it was only Bone's."

Brenda sent out a telepathic thought. "Bone scuffed it with his shoes. He was very angry."

Doris blinked. "Bone scuffed it with his shoes," she said. "He was very angry."

At that moment, Jim's torchbeam picked out something on the corner of the ruined painting. "Look, gang." He bent to pick up the blue clump of waftiness. "Feathers!"

"Rerk, let me see." Doris hop-fluttered up onto his

shoulder and inspected the clump. "No, by my beak, they aren't feathers. Not real ones, at least. They're artificial. Hmmph!"

Jim rubbed the glossy blueness between his fingers. "So they are," he said, screwing up his nose.

"Quaaaooo!" came Brenda's urgent snort.

"Yes, my lovely, I know. But there's no need to be alarmed too much. Tastelessness such as this can be found everywhere nowadays—"

"*Quaaaoooo!*"

"It's all right, Bren," soothed Doris, holding up a wing. "I still have the genuine thing. Don't worry, I'm still the real macaw."

"*QUAAAAOOOOO!*" Brenda snorted loudly, in her best I'm-not-disturbed-by-the-artificial-feathers-but-listen-to-that-noise! tone.

"Erk," said Doris. "I don't think it's the artificial feathers that're worrying her."

"Listen," implored the Wonder Camel telepathically.

"Shh!" whispered Jim. "Listen, she's heard something."

Doris cocked her head, squawkless.

Jim leaned his neck forward, wordless.

Brenda's nostrils opened widely, snortless.

Slowly and faintly, as though it was coming from a time that had been smothered by cobwebs, a noise was rising beneath them.

A voice, thin and soft and hesitant.

Cairo Jim turned towards a rectangular hole in the

floor, near the left-hand wall of the Temple. His torch-light moved across the floor, and then disappeared into the hole.

"It's coming from down there," he whispered, the hairs on the back of his legs standing on end. "From the tomb of King Pakal!"

♠♠♠♠♠ **11** ♠♠♠♠♠

IN THE TOMB OF KING PAKAL

"RERK!" BLINKED DORIS, digging her claws into Jim's shirt. "What is it, Jim?"

"Only one way to find out. C'mon, Brenda, very quietly."

Doris gulped.

They moved closer to the hole and peered down. A series of roughly hewn steps – much rougher than the ones on the outside of the Temple – swept away into the pitch darkness.

"Listen," mouthed Jim.

The sound stopped for a few moments. All the trio could hear was the muffled noises of the jungle outside, and a dripping of water from somewhere deep within the Temple.

Then the voice came back.

"Sounds like singing," cooed Doris quietly.

"Mmm," said Jim.

"Quaaoo," snorted Brenda.

Doris was right – it *did* sound like singing. A single voice, lonely and shimmery, trailing away and starting tunelessly again, coming from deep within the tomb:

"*Happy days … are the days … I like to gaze …*

on yesterdays ... hip, hip hoorays ... and no delays ...
give me happy, happy days..."

"Doesn't sound like *Bone*," Jim said.

"Doesn't sound human," blinked Doris.

"Let's go down and find out what's there."

Doris's crest arched forward. "Go down there? Into a *tomb*?"

"We might find something we need," answered Jim. "We've got barely any clues as to where to find Bone. Besides, you've been in tombs before, my dear. What about the Valley of the Kings?"

"But, Jim." Doris was flexing up and down on his shoulder. "Those tombs were *huge*. You know how I hate enclosed spaces that are *small*."

"Brenda and I'll be with you."

"But what if it's ... what if it's a *spirit*?"

Jim looked at her.

"What if it's *Pakal* himself?"

"Then maybe we can teach him some more up-to-date tunes to sing for the rest of Eternity." He gave her a wink, a wide wink that he hoped appeared to be filled with confidence, even though his heart was fluttering like a million over-excited butterflies.

Doris wrapped a wing around his neck. Jim could feel her feathers trembling slightly. "I'm with you, Jim," she squerked. "Always."

"*Happy days ... are the days ... I like to gaze ... on yesterdays..."*

A zinging shiver shot through Jim's and Doris's spines.

"Quaaaoooo!" Brenda gave a snort of reassurance.

"Yes, my lovely," smiled Jim. "You're right. Even if it *is* a spirit, there're three of us, aren't there? And only one of it."

The Wonder Camel rotated her head in a wide circle.

"Let's descend, then," whispered the archaeologist-poet, leading the way.

The walls of the narrow passage leading down from the floor of the Temple were cool and moist to the touch. Jim and Brenda had to be careful when they placed boots and hoofs on each step; some were nothing more than chunks of uneven rock, their nobbly edges having been worn away by countless pairs of tourists' feet during the daylight hours.

As they descended, and as their torchlights bobbed off the rough walls and steps and into the impenetrable blackness below, the singing came and went, rising and falling on the gloom around them.

"*… and no delays … happy, happy days…*"

The dank walls seemed to absorb the tune and bounce it back again, making it echo uncertainly around the gloomy passage.

"Whoops," gasped Jim, as his boot slid on the worn steps. Doris fluttered her wings harshly to try and help him regain his balance. Their torchlights danced crazily up and down the walls.

"Steady on, Jim of Cairo," thought Brenda, behind him.

The archaeologist-poet straightened his back and,

with gritted teeth and gritted eyebrows, proceeded downwards.

The stairs came to an end. As Jim, Doris and Brenda reached the level floor of the tomb, the singing came to an end also.

"Jim?" Doris asked warily.

He took a deep breath and pointed his torch into the darkness. "Hello?" he called, his voice struggling to get out of his throat.

There was no answer.

Brenda's eyelashes tingled with a creeping fear.

"Anybody there?" Jim called again, moving his light around the walls. Slowly the beam passed across the gigantic oblong sarcophagus of King Pakal, making the orange-coloured stone appear a murky yellow.

But still there was no answer.

"Maybe whatever it was has evaporated," suggested Doris. "Faded away. Perhaps we scared it off."

Jim opened his mouth to comment on her thought, but he uttered no sound: the silence was broken by a distant cackle, dissolving away like water down a plug-hole.

"Ha ha ha ha ha ha ha haaaeeeerrrrgghhhh!"

Every follicle of Brenda's hairs, every fibre of Doris's feathers, every pore in Cairo Jim's skin jumped with a million volts of startledness.

Then came another sound: the echo of footsteps, loud and slapping, disappearing into the void.

"Hear that?" blurted Jim, his voice still quavering

from the onslaught of the unknown. "*Spirits* don't make sounds like that. Those are human feet!"

"Rerk, look! Up ahead!"

There was a flash of whiteness, a *flowing* flash of whiteness, that disappeared around a corner.

"After it!" Brenda urged telepathically.

"Come on," hissed Jim, "after it!"

With careful steps they pursued the white thing around the corner. Then they stopped abruptly.

"Dead end," squawked the macaw, beaming her light into every corner of the short corridor they had entered.

"Well, swoggle me suddenly," muttered Cairo Jim.

"Quaaaooo!" Brenda jerked her snout-held torch towards the far wall. The Wonder Camel had seen a tiny, paper-thin crack in the wall, which had been opened for a split second, and which had then disappeared completely.

Jim had seen it too, thanks to her snorting warning, and through the opened crack he had glimpsed a darkness that was less thick than the darkness that was smothering them inside the tomb.

"What?" Doris flapped. "What is it?"

Slowly Jim approached the wall, illuminating the area where the crack had been. "Just for a second, there was a chink in the stones. Here, running horizontally along the wall. And through it we saw the night outside."

"Preeerrrk!"

Brenda and Doris watched as Jim ran his fingers

along the surface. "Ah! Here it is! My goodness, it's so very fine you can hardly see it." With a sweating index finger he traced the line all the way along to the right – about one and a half metres – until it stopped. "Wait a minute," he whispered. "Look, it changes direction. See, here it starts going down to the floor." He crouched and ran his finger all the way down to his boots.

"Quaaaooo."

"Coo. Secret panel, Jim?"

Jim stood again and moved across to the left-hand side, where he found the line travelling down to the floor there also. "Looks like," he muttered.

"Looks like our spirit did 'choose out some secret place, some reverend room'," said Doris, quoting from *King Richard II*.

"Seems as though our spirit did," frowned Jim. "Now if we can only find a way to get there ourselves." He stepped back from the panel and they all three shone their lights across it. "There's got to be *some* way to open it…"

Brenda fluttered her eyelashes and sucked all her breath deeply in, in, in and further in, until she was considerably slimmer. Then, with a slow and steady circular motion, she turned herself completely around (Jim, with Doris on his shoulder, stepped as far out of the way as he could in the narrow passageway), being careful not to brush the sides of her humps against the clammy walls.

"Hey, Bren, this is no time for dancing!"

"Sh, my dear, I think she's up to something."

They both watched silently as Brenda reversed up to the panel in the wall. Delicately she raised her tail and, in notable Wonder Camel fashion, she snapped it straight so that it was as rigid as a stick.

"Doris," whispered Jim, "I've only ever seen her do this once before, when we needed to paint an urgent sign to warn the villagers of Gurna that Neptune Bone had been swimming naked in the Gurna swimming pool—"

"Yergh!" Doris winced her beak.

"Look, she's doing it again!"

Without a sound, all of the hairs at the end of Brenda's tail drooped down like withered petals on a dying rose. But only for a moment – for, immediately after, they rose again, majestically up to the top of her stiffened tail, and snapped themselves to attention, into an *absolutely perfect and very fine point.*

Doris gasped, and Cairo Jim smiled.

The Wonder Camel wiggled her hind portions about, and her tail fell into a horizontal position. Then the point on the tip of her tail began to move slowly across all the stones that were bordered by the cracks. With the newly shaped point, she was able to probe into every minuscule nook, every miniature cranny, every almost-nonexistent hole and gap.

"QUAAAAOOOO!" she snorted at last. She jiggled her tailpoint in a tiny opening – no deeper than a blowfly's throat – and pulled her tail out, swishing it triumphantly into the air.

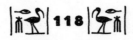

She moved away from the wall, and the scraping sound of rock against rock ground into the passageway. With a gravelly groaning, the panel swivelled towards Jim, Doris and Brenda, to reveal shadows of the outside, night-time world.

"Quick," Doris screeched, "before it closes again! These things aren't known to stay open for ever!"

In a blink of time they all ducked through the opening, Brenda clip-clopping backwards.

"My lovely, you are brilliant!" Jim reached over and stroked her mane with great warmth. She fluttered her eyelashes appreciatively and let all the air out from her insides, gradually returning to her normal shape.

Doris hopped onto her head and gave her a soft peck between her ears. "Good one, Bren."

Jim ran his torchlight across the ground. "As we thought. See, those prints are from sandals. We're following a human, all right." He shone the light into the jungle. "And I'm pretty sure it's not Bone. He'd never be seen dead in white."

Up ahead, some bushes quivered at the edge of the pool of light from Brenda's torch.

"Rark!" fluttered Doris. "Over there!"

They waved their lights across the undergrowth, and more bushes shook, this time a bit further away.

"Come on," whispered Jim. "Let's not lose whoever it is."

Through the foliage they rushed, shining their torches on the palm fronds and vine-encrusted boughs before them, hurrying past great boulders that were riddled with intricate but bold patterns of algae and mosses. Doris held on to Jim's shoulder tightly for fear that the slapping branches around them would knock her off.

For five minutes they followed the shaking bushes and disturbed palm fronds. The jungle was getting thicker; what had been a sort of rough trail was now smothered by the gloom of night-time greenery, and the three of them had to slow their pace considerably.

The shaking of the surrounding undergrowth became harder to spot in the thick gloom; the sound of swishing leaves less regular.

Until it stopped completely.

Jim came to a halt, as did Brenda behind him. They waited, breathing loudly, for a sign of their "spirit".

Then Jim spoke, after what seemed like an eternity of waiting: "Well, I guess we lost it."

"I guess *we're* lost, too," squawked Doris with annoyance. She flew from Jim's shoulder and waddled about on the soft, damp-smelling ground.

"Quaaaooo," snorted Brenda uncertainly.

Jim looked all around. "No, my dear, we're not lost. We came that way..." He took off his pith helmet and rubbed the top of his left ear. "I think."

"Rark, no we didn't. We came from over there!"

"No," thought Brenda, "the Temple of the Inscriptions is back over yonder."

"Hmm," grimaced the archaeologist-poet. "This trip

seems to be amounting to nothing but riddles." He went to the nearest large rock and sat heavily. "We're getting nowhere with finding Bone and Mademoiselle Glusac. We don't even know what his motive is for kidnapping her, or what he's after." With a click, he turned off his torch.

"I wish we could've caught that ... that ... whatever it was," Doris conjectured. "It must've thought we were going to do it some harm or something."

"That we'd never do," Jim said. "Just a few questions, that's all..."

"That's what the other güero said," came a thin voice that sounded like it was shimmering on a moonbeam.

"Quaaaooo!" snorted Brenda.

Jim jumped up as if a skyrocket had just been let off straight up the back of his shirt.

Doris's crest arched forward until it almost covered her eyes.

"Hello?" called Jim, peering all around. "Hello? Please come out. We only want to talk with you. We don't want anything else."

The following seconds were filled, *overflowing*, with silence.

No breeze wafted.

No droplets of dew settled.

Not even any creatures of the jungle were stirring.

No life at all.

Until ...

A face, old and leathery in the moonlight and

framed by a tangly border of pure white hair, poked out through the foliage.

The old man's lips curled up at the corners and his eyes glinted warily. "No?" came the shimmery voice.

Brenda reared up slightly, and Jim reached quickly over and grabbed her bridle to bring her back to earth. "No," he answered. "Nothing more at all. We'd just like to ask you some questions. You see, we're on a bit of a quest."

The old one eyed him shrewdly.

"We're looking for something," Jim went on, "or rather, some *one* ... no, I mean, some *ones* who ... oh, swoggle me swiftly with a sombrero, this is so hard to explain."

The old man moved slowly forward, and emerged from the leafy growth. Now Jim, Doris and Brenda could see him fully and unobscured.

His long white hair flowed gently down from his head, and spilled across his shoulders with a forlorn softness. He was dressed in a pure white smock that hung from his thin shoulders almost all the way down to his ankles. On his feet he wore a pair of sandals that looked as if they had been woven and plaited from flax or reeds. Around his neck was a long, slender cord, laced with leaves and straggly strips of vivid woven material which hung down in a loop across his narrow chest.

Slung across his shoulder was an old, well-oiled bow. If Jim, Doris and Brenda could have seen the old man's back at this moment, they would have seen the long, cylindrical tube, made from the bark of a rubber tree and containing six arrows with brightly feathered tails, attached with vine-straps to his smock.

"Then, if it is only *answers* that you seek, come with me."

12
ONWARDS WITH A VENGEANCE

MEANWHILE, MANY MILES to the east, a dark blue Bugatti was motoring speedily towards the site of the ancient civilisation of Chichén Itzá.

The driver was wearing one of his touring fezzes – this one the colour of shortbread, with a wisteria-hued tassel – and smoking his Belch of Brouhaha cigar with an earnest and determined anger.

Next to him, the flea-infested bundle of ill-assorted black feathers was throwing her beak back regularly and laughing raucously – in the way that certain types of birds do – to the night-time wind.

While in the back seat, a platinum-blonde-haired and slightly cross-eyed cabaret artiste was staring at the roadway ahead and making loud, what-a-waste-of-time type sounds by clicking her tongue against the upper realms of the inside of her mouth.

The Bugatti surged onwards.

The raven laughed onwards.

The cabaret artiste scoffed onwards.

The driver fumed onwards, in a cloud of derisive fury.

"*Chugga-chugga-chugga-chugga!*"

"*Ha-crark-ha-crark-ha-crark-ha!*"

"*Tch-tch-tch-tch-tch-tch-tch!*"

"*Arr, arr, arr, arr, arr, arr, AAAAARRRRR!*"

13

ARMANDO'S TALE

EVEN THOUGH IT WAS NOW very dark in the jungles of Palenque, the white-haired, white-clothed old man was able to find his way through the gloomy foliage without any difficulty or confusion.

He led Jim, Doris and Brenda deeper into the rustling and swaying thickness of leaves, vines and ancient tree trunks, past heavily hidden, crumbling stone walls that had been built long ago and which appeared to be still standing only because of the enormous tree roots that had sprouted and grown fat between the stones.

(Many of these tree roots were as thick as a grown man's waist, and Cairo Jim thought that they appeared to fork down to the damp earth like mighty fingers balancing the remainder of a gigantic – though invisible – body.)

"Rark," rarked Doris at one point as she shone her torch across a moss-covered wall. "Where are we, Jim? What *is* this place?"

"Probably used to be the outskirts of the city. All of this hasn't been excavated yet." The archaeologist-poet cast his beam up one of the walls, across the deeper darkness made by a Mayan arch doorway, and onto a row of block-shaped, small towers that had once been

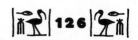

the roof-comb crowning this overgrown dwelling. Now, thick bushes oozed out between the rectangular holes in each roof-comb, and much of the carved stucco facades were heavily pasted with dark and velvety mosses.

"Back where we just came from – the Temple of Inscriptions and Pakal's Tomb and the Palace and all those other buildings – all of that area's been cleared away. Before the great archaeologist Alberto Ruz Lhuillier started excavating in 1945, it was smothered by the jungle, just like these buildings are. But all of *this*, here further into the forest, hasn't been touched by human hands in the last 1200 years. This is how much of those other buildings back there would've looked when the site was discovered."

"Quaaaooo," snorted Brenda, imagining the scene.

"I wonder," pondered Jim aloud, "whether any archaeologists or explorers have even *been* this far off the beaten track since Alberto Ruz Lhuillier 'found' Palenque. I wonder if they know this exists."

At this, the old man in white, who had been walking softly ahead but within earshot, turned and gave Cairo Jim a smile. Then he turned back, wordlessly, to their route.

After nearly half an hour more of ducking beneath low branches and edging around the corners of neglected stone barriers, the old man in white led them all down a thickly ferned slope that was cathedralled above by a dense overhanging of bending tree branches, interlaced with a criss-crossing network of gnarled and tightly knotted vines.

At the bottom of this slope – darker than anywhere they had so far stumbled upon in the forest – were a few stone walls. As Jim was going down the slope, he flashed his torchlight across the walls and saw that they were sprouting with small, leafy twigs and ferns growing through the cracks between the stones. Much of the masonry had crumbled or had been pushed apart by the greenery, so that the stones were no taller than knee-high, but at the back of the area there were three walls still substantially standing.

Above these walls, where they all met to form a small, partly enclosed, cabaña-like shelter, there was a roughly thatched roof made from huge leaves and coarse palm-tree fronds.

The man in white reached the semi-clearing at the bottom of the slope, with the naturally formed canopy of protection above. Slowly he turned, opening his arms wide. "This my home," he said in his moonbeam tone. "You are welcome here."

And then, before Jim, Doris or Brenda could make a sound, he wafted off into the enclosed cabaña at the back of the clearing.

Jim cast his light at the hut, through the darkness that seemed to be buzzing about like a cloud of frantic and befuddled insects.

Gradually a faint glow of light swelled from within the cabaña, becoming brighter and brighter. In a few moments the old man emerged, holding aloft a small kerosene lantern.

"Please forgive the state of things," he said. "I rarely get visitors." Their host came back to the centre of the clearing and set the lantern on a big, flattish rock. "I will answer your questions as best as I can."

"Thank you," said Jim. He switched off his torch, and Doris and Brenda did likewise.

"But first, would you like some food? I have a monkey that I shot some days ago..." He unlooped the tube of arrows from his back and the bow from his shoulder, and dumped them both on the ground. "By now it should be ready for roasting."

"Rark!" squawked Doris, and Brenda rolled her head in the negative.

"No, no thank you," replied Jim hastily. "But thank you for the thought."

"You are welcome." The old man smiled, his leathery face folding into a hundred new creases. "Please, sit."

He sat first, cross-legged.

Jim followed, with Doris on his shoulder. When he had settled, she hopped off and onto a pile of leaves by his side. Brenda lowered herself in a naturally ceremonious fashion that was common to camels from the Wonder Herd of Thebes.

"Please," Jim said when they were all comfortable, "tell us who you are."

"Ah!" The old man raised his hand, palm outwards, as if he were asking to be pardoned. "Of course. My name is Armando. Armando Tezzistecoátl. I am the last of my people."

"What people are they?" blinked Doris.

"*Were* they," corrected Armando Tezzistecoátl. "We *were* of a tribe of which you would not have ever heard. A people who were breathing the air from many long times past." His eyes glazed over and his smile softened, until it was nothing more than the *ghost* of the smile that had previously been on his lips. Then the words to his song – the same words that had risen up from the dark depths of Pakal's tomb – flowed out of his mouth in a whisper of wistfulness:

"*Happy days … are the days … I like to gaze … on yesterdays … hip, hip hoorays … and no delays … give me happy, happy days…*"

Cairo Jim took off his pith helmet and wiped his eyebrows with his left wrist. "Tell us, Armando, what happened to your people?"

The old man licked his rough lips and stared at the lantern. "Today got them," he answered slowly.

"Today?" Doris echoed, opening and closing her wings.

"Si. Today, and all the things that all of today has brought with it. Everything started falling apart when the men came to take away the forest from all of those buildings that today's people call Palenque. Before this, my people had lived there, in the overgrown buildings, very happily. There was quiet, and peace, and many, many animals to hunt. When the moon shone full, the walls of the Palace were white, like mist that refuses to move. The water was always sweet and fresh. But when the men came to clear away the jungle from our home, we had to flee."

"And you moved further into the jungle?" asked Jim.

Armando nodded. "I did, along with a few others. But not everyone. Many of the younger men were curious about what the intruders were doing. At first the younger men of our tribe came into the jungle with us, but soon they started disappearing during the day. I found out they were going back to Palenque to watch all the intruders and their big machines and their tiny scientific gadgets. After a time, our younger men became bolder, until one of them actually approached the boss of the intruders and made his acquaintance. The boss-intruder offered him a job, as part of the team, and then he offered the other young men from our tribe the same sorts of jobs. I heard that our young men were very valuable to the intruders, because of their knowledge of the buildings and the country around here.

"Then, after years of digging and cutting and removing the green arms of our homes, the work was done. Palenque was ready for more intruders, to come and walk across the staircases and stare in awe at the majesty of our forebears. Palenque was ready for the touristos.

"It was time for the first lot of intruders to leave; their job was done. Many of our young men had become so like these intruders – with their today ways and their scientific gadgets – that they were invited to leave with them. To go to the city, or to other parts of the forest to find other places like Palenque. And so our young men went. They moved on, with the taste of today fresh in their mouths, and the thought of yesterday a cobweb in their minds.

"I was left here with the few others who chose the jungle. But, as the years have passed, and the things of today have squeezed out the things of yesterday, my tribespeople have moved on too. In different ways, they have all moved on. Now, only *I* remain." He sighed – a big, hollow sigh that stretched his ribcage. "It is so sad when you lose your people like this."

Brenda gave a quiet snort ... she knew *exactly* what Armando was saying.

"Yes," nodded Cairo Jim.

"And so," smiled Armando, "I spend my days here, far away from the surge of the touristos. I hunt and scavenge in the jungle, and keep chopping back the vines before they swallow my home. But when the sun begins to go down, I go back. There. To Palenque. I am very careful to get there just as the last of the touristos are leaving ... what a good thing that Palenque closes to those people at sunset. Then, the whole place is mine once again! Sometimes I take my lantern and sometimes, if the moon is strong, I do not. Do you know what I do when I get there?"

"What?" asked Doris.

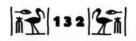

"I go *prowling*. Like the jaguar I sometimes see through the thick, green leaves. I go looking around, all over the buildings, anywhere that the touristos have been. And I find the things that they have left behind, the things that are of *today*, but for those who left them behind will be *yesterday's* memories and nothing more."

"Do you find many things?" Jim asked.

"Oh, you would not believe the things I have found in all the years I have been on the prowl. Beautiful combs to brush the hair. Books – many books – full of pictures of Palenque and other places in Mexico that the touristos go to. Other sorts of books, too, big thick books with paper covers and no pictures but lots of words, telling stories of nurses and detectives and mysterious things." He jerked his thumb back towards his small cabaña. "I have my own *biblioteca* – you call it 'library' – thanks to all those books!"

This made Jim feel good.

"And there are many other things. Wallets of leather, full of little glossy cards that are no use to me. Many tin cans, which I pick up and put in a pile, because when they are strewn around they make ugliness. Pesos and American dollars. Metal keys on chains. An artificial leg. Sun-spectacles of the most curious design. Once I even found a bag full of vacuum-cleaner bits and pieces that had been left behind after a convention of vacuum-cleaner sellers had visited the place.

"But the most important find I have made on my prowlings – the one which has brought me so much repeated happiness – happened many years ago. This is what I brought the other güero★ to see."

"Yes," Jim said with polite urgency. "You mentioned this 'other güero' before. Could you tell us what he looked like, Armando?"

At this request, Armando rolled his eyes. "Never have I seen such a collection of clothing on the one man! Sometimes, when I am feeling very reckless, I will go *before* sunset to the edge of Palenque, and crouch in the bushes and watch the touristos as they are leaving. This is how I can speak other languages; I pick it up from the touristos. They wear some strange clothes, si?"

"That they do," nodded Jim of Cairo, thrumming his fingers on the top of his pith helmet which was resting on his knees.

"But *this* güero … it was a sight to behold. He was a hut of a man, not tall, but big in this direction" – Armando held both arms wide – "and he wore a short, stubby hat, the colour of spearmint grass, with a short tail of cochineal-coloured hair hanging from it."

"Quaaaooo!" Brenda snorted with distaste at the awful mess of colours.

"A fez, all right!" squawked Doris.

"And," Armando went on, "he smoked a smelly thick cigarro and wore a coat with no sleeves, bright green, and a shirt that looked like a salamander had walked in paint and run around all over it."

★ A fair-complexioned person who is not a Mexican.

"His shirts are louder than the Cairo Brass Band," Doris flapped.

"And his trousers ended at his fatty knees – those trousers were too tight for my liking, especially around his backside – and under the knees, all the way to his black-and-white shoes, he wore hairy stockings decorated with oranges and lemons. I do not know if the hairs were part of his stockings or were poking through from his legs."

Cairo Jim had listened silently, his jaw setting into a rigid vice of dread and loathing. "Armando, did he have anyone else with him?"

"Si, si, he did. A bird, black and filthy, with throbbing eyes the colour of blood, who was always pecking at itself and spitting things out—"

"Raaark!" shuddered Doris.

"—and a senorita, very thin, wearing a headdress of fake quetzal feathers ... I could tell they were fake because they were stiff and wonky, not natural and flowing like the real feathers of this beautiful bird."

"Fifi Glusac," Jim muttered.

"She had green dingle-dangles hanging from her ears and her nose. And I remember," Armando added, "that her eyes were slightly crossed, just like the senorita in the painting that someone had done very recently in the Temple of the Inscriptions. Another sign of today that we could well do without!"

Cairo Jim began to tingle: now, at last, for the first time since he, Doris and Brenda had actually arrived in Mexico, he knew that they were on the right track.

"Armando," he said eagerly, "it seems that we know this man. And we have to find him quickly, for he's up to some kind of typical monumental rottenness."

"Ah, I would believe it! He was very impatient with me when I found him at Palenque. Demanding and impatient."

"What did he want with you?"

Armando sighed. "I still do not know. He acted like he was Montezuma himself!"

Jim frowned.

"He greeted me, then started babbling on about some sort of ... what did he call it? Ah, si, I remember: some sort of *invaluable treasure* that I might have hidden away somewhere. He said that the Quetzal Queen had returned for it, because it belonged to her. This is when he pointed to the thin senorita with the stiff and wonky fake feathers on her head."

"Did you know what he was talking about?" Jim asked, leaning forward.

"Not at first, no. But then he told me that this invaluable treasure was very old, and that I would have had it for a long time. Then I realised what he meant! So I bring him here to show it to him and to the filthy bird and the cross-eyed senorita."

"Rark! What did you show them?"

"Come, come, I will show you all, too."

With a creak, Armando stood and straightened out his white smock. Jim and Brenda stood also and Doris fluttered up onto Brenda's fore hump. Then Armando picked up the lantern and led them all to the door-hole of his small cabaña.

"Wait here, and I'll get it ready for you," he whispered intriguingly.

He ducked into the cabaña, and there was a very loud sound. CRIIICCCKKK ... CRIIICCCKKK ... CRIIICCCKKK ...

Jim looked at Brenda, Brenda at Doris on her hump, and Doris back at Jim.

"Enter," called Armando.

In they went, to see the white-clothed back of Armando as he bent over something. And then, as though it were coming from many years ago and travelling across moonbeams of time, a scratchy, thin sound rose forth, fuzzy at times and clear at times.

"Music," whispered Doris.

"Music?" whispered Jim.

"Music," she cooed.

Then came words, sailing along on the forgotten tune:

"Happy days ... are the days ... I like to gaze ... on yesterdays ... hip, hip hoorays ... and no delays ... give me happy, happy days..."

Armando moved aside and Jim, Doris and Brenda saw the music-maker: a very old wind-up gramophone with a small funnel-shaped speaker attached to the top.

"This is my best piece of prowling finding," announced Armando, watching the scratched record slowly turning around. "I found it one day many years ago, just sitting by itself on the grass, near the Temple of the Count at Palenque. I reason that some people were having a picnic or something, and they left in a hurry. Now this is my *invaluable treasure!*"

"*Hip, hip hoorays … and no delays … give me happy, happy days…*"

The words sounded melancholy, as though all of today's claws were trying to grasp back through time itself and scratch the song away.

"Tell me," said Jim, "what did this strangely dressed man do when you presented the gramophone to him?"

"Oh, well, I was very troubled by his reaction. He really flipped his lid. He thundered out of my cabaña in a dark rage, and screamed many words that I hope I never have to hear again. He dragged the filthy bird by its throat, and the senorita by her wrist, and went back off into the night, yelling rude names. As he disappeared off through the trees, I heard him shouting something about Chichén Itzá."

"That makes some sort of sense," Jim observed. "The paintings of the Quetzal Queen have also appeared there."

"But I think," smiled Armando, "that he is wasting his time going to Chichén Itzá."

"Quaaaaoooo?" thought Brenda.

"Why?" flapped Doris. "Why's he wasting his time?"

"Well, he told me that he was looking for some thing that was invaluable treasure, si? Something that once belonged to this Quetzal Queen?"

"Si," said Jim. "I mean, yes."

"Now, after he had left I remembered about the Quetzal Queen. I remembered how my mother had told me about this wonderful Queen when I was a very young muchacho. Would you know, I hadn't had a single thought about her since I was very little – the Quetzal Queen, I mean, not my mother – but now that this rude man had mentioned her again, all the stories my mother told me came flooding back. About how she reigned for nearly eight hundred years, without ever growing old or wrinkled or sad. Ah! I even remembered *where* she reigned!"

"Where?" asked Cairo Jim, almost breathlessly.

"My mother told me that she had her Palace at a place called Uxmal. They say that there she kept the secret of her youthfulness."

Suddenly every bit of Cairo Jim ran cold. His eyes unfocussed for the briefest of moments, and his knees nearly buckled under him.

"Rark!" Doris screeched. "Jim, are you all right? Are you going to faint?"

Jim shook his head and took a deep breath. "Swoggle me eternally, over and over and over," he moaned. "It appears that Bone's after the very thing that no one's ever been able to find!"

The gramophone had wound down, and now only a few slow and drawn-out words came from the speaker:

"… *giiiive meeee haaaaapppppppy hhhaaaaaaaaaapppppppy daaaaaaaaaayyyyyyyyyyssssssssss…*"

Jim turned to Armando. "You say he's wasting his time going off to Chichén Itzá?"

"Why, si. I never heard of the Quetzal Queen living there at all."

"For some reason Bone doesn't seem to know that. That's good; it means we can have a headstart on him and hopefully get to Uxmal before he does. Armando, can you remember if your mother knew *where* at Uxmal this … this *invaluable treasure* that kept the Queen so young … was stored?"

The old man shook his head slowly. "No. I don't think anyone but the local Indians who live around Uxmal know."

"Quuuaaaaoooooo!" Brenda snorted in her there's-not-a-moment-to-be-wasted tone. Doris started jerking up and down impatiently.

"Armando, do you mind if we leave in a hurry? Right now?" Jim put on his pith helmet again and straightened his socks, pulling them up from his boots.

"No, I do not. *Sea rápido, adiós.* Go, and see what you can find. Do not worry about me," he smiled, "for I will be around for a long time to come."

▲▲▲▲▲ 14 ▲▲▲▲▲

AT THE PYRAMID OF KUKULCÁN

"Things I Shall Do In My Next Two Hundred Years."

Captain Neptune Flannelbottom Bone sat in a collapsible director's chair he had erected on the top platform of the massive, cloud-scraping Pyramid of Kukulcán, the most colossal Mayan structure at Chichén Itzá. Into a parchment-papered writing pad in his wide lap he had scribbled the above heading and now, as dusk began to settle, he lifted his eyes from the pad and gazed out across the wide plains and into the surrounding scrub, while he puffed indulgently on his cigar.

His fury at having his time wasted by what he called "that stupid little hovel-dwelling man in the white nightie with the pathetic taste in modern music" had gradually evaporated away, like a thinning fog of bitterness. Now the over-dressed Captain was slightly calmer. Now he was slightly more certain of his future. Now he was much more anxious than ever to get his pudgy fingers on the Elixir of Eternity – his invaluable treasure – and begin the rest of his life.

A small breeze danced up the procession of stairs and blew against the fleshy man, causing the cigar smoke to swirl back into his beard. Bone screwed up

his nose and muttered, "Arrrrr." Then, beneath the heading in his pad, he scribbled:

> "1. *Harness the wind so that it shall blow*
> *only where I wish it to blow.*"

He gave a self-satisfied humph and looked down the almost endless sequence of steps, and he had a small but wobbly shudder as he remembered how hard they had been to climb. He had not sweated so much since he had accidentally got his nose stuck in the keyhole of the Bold Pussycat Ping-Pong Club for Millionairesses three years ago in Dubai.[*] By the time he had reached the top of this pyramid's northern staircase, he was drenched with so much sweat that he felt wetter than when he had gone diving in the Red Sea, and now his natural prune-like body odour was more heavy and cloying.

He screwed up his nose once again – not at his body odour, but at the thought of how the stairs had forced him to use up so much energy – and scribbled:

> "2. *Eliminate all the stairs of the world.*"

---

[*] If it hadn't been for the (for once) quick thinking of Desdemona, who had dribbled a stream of ravengoo all over his nose and forehead and chin, thereby lubricating his nose and allowing him to slip it out of the keyhole, he might still be there today.

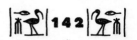

From inside the temple behind him, a muffled thunk-thunk-thunking sound was coming. Bone turned his head and called loudly at the stone wall. "Keep searching, Desdemona. There could be a rotating panel anywhere in there."

A muffled croak of bad words came from within the temple.

Bone felt the stirrings of inspiration inside his belly and, pausing only to puff self-importantly on the cigar, he scrawled more plans in rapid succession:

"*3. Declare all banks shall be as one, and will be known as the Bone World Bank (n.b. this will take some time, but what care I?)*

4. Eradicate tofu forever.

5. Destroy all jungles, rainforests and cloudforests on account of their sinisterness.

6. Prevent children from speaking until they are eighteen years of age.

7. Set up a global gold repository to be known as Fort Bone.

8. Outlaw the Old Relics Society and declare the profession of archaeologist to be illegal.

9. Annihilate Cairo Jim and his goody-two-humps camel and that feathered monstrosity Doris.

10. Give a small portion of the Elixir of Eternity to Jocelyn Osgood of Valkyrian Airways and crown her as my eternal Queen (though she will not by any means be equal to me).

11. Ban the Antiquities Squad.

12. Become Ruler of the Earth."

He adjusted his mulberry-coloured fez with the tangerine tassel and smirked as he beheld his plans. "Arrr," he arrred contentedly. He folded the pad and shoved it into the tight back pocket of his plus-fours trousers. Then he pulled down his waistcoat, raised his arms above his head, locked his manicured fingers together and stretched out until all his knuckles cracked like pistol shots.

Time would soon be in his grasp, he told himself, and then it would be his *slave*.

He sat for a while with his hands clasped behind his head, watching the sky changing from a bold pink to a thick, rich mauve.

And then the sound of wings behind him – huge wings, powerful wings, wings coming at him through the centuries of forgetfulness – plunged the temperature of his bloodstream to ice.

"*WHOOOSH, WHOOOSH, WHOOOSH!*"

He leapt heavily from his chair, flinging his cigar to the limestone floor beneath him, and turned around to face the flapping. His forehead poured with perspiration and his cheeks turned the colour of chalk.

Out of the temple, in a flurry of annoyance and anger, hurtled Desdemona through the air. She came to a skidding halt by Bone's feet.

"Crarrrk! Nevermore, nevermore, nevermore!"

"It's … it's only *you*?" stammered Bone, his many folds of fat trembling.

"Of course it's only me. Who'dja expect, Mahatma Gandhi?"

"You sounded like…" He whipped out his grubby silk handkerchief and mopped the wetness from his brow. "Never mind, it must've been the echo inside there."

"Sounded like *who*?" asked Desdemona, her eyes throbbing with curiosity.

"Never you mind, you abdominous article of atrociousness." A faraway look came across his face and he muttered quietly, "Never shall I return to Greece, not in a *thousand* lifetimes."

The raven hopped up onto the director's chair and made herself at home, rubbing her bent beak with one wing and plucking fleas from her upperbits with the other. "There's no secret panel in there, I'm here to tell you," she rasped. "No concealed passageways, no sliding doors, no nothing. Only a lot of bats' droppings and cobwebs and a couple of vacuum-cleaner brochures that someone's dropped. I think there've been a few people through here … your Quetzal Queen painting's been walked all over."

"The onslaught of the tourists," sneered Bone, now back to his old self. "Where's La Stupido?"

"Having a wander down there, near the Temple of a Thousand Columns. She took off. I made her. She kept trying to stroke my feathers and I told her if she didn't vamoose and let me get on with my important work I'd relieve her of a few toes. Crark! I'll do that anyway, after she's served her purpose with us. Ha-crark-haaaa!"

Bone said nothing at this, but took out his silver cigar-lighter from his waistcoat pocket and a wad of straw and linen strips from under the chair. He twisted the wad tight and placed it into a hole in the wall of the temple. With a flick of his cigar-lighter he set the wad alight, and it began to burn slowly, but with a bright flame. "This might entice the locals out," he muttered, casting his gaze downwards, hoping to see similar blazing torchlights emerging through the bush.

For the moment, however, the dusk was the only sort of light visible, and it sat heavily over the earth like a suspended blanket.

"Captain," Desdemona croaked as she hop-fluttered onto the wooden armrest of the chair, "tell me something."

"What is it you wish to know, you questioning quagmire of queerness?"

"Why did we have to bring that La Stupido dame on this trip? I don't get it."

Bone sighed and, puffing loudly, bent over to retrieve his cigar from the stones. He put it to his broad lips and sucked and puffed quickly until the nearly extinguished cigar was fully lit again. "There's a perfectly good reason, Desdemona. We need her for her talents."

"What, you mean because she's a bit cross-eyed? What's so special about that? I wouldn't have thought that being cross-eyed was a big deal. It only lands you in trouble."

"Whatever are you droning about?"

"Take that play *Romeo and Juliet*, by that Shakespeare feller. I saw it once, at an open-air production in Cairo. I didn't pay of course, just swooped on in. In that play, it says 'a pair of cross-eyed lovers take their life'. Doesn't sound very successful to me, being cross-eyed."

"That's 'star-crossed lovers', you feathered, fully flead fool! And if you don't stop your stupidity, you'll be a *boot*-crossed bird!"

"Well why did you choose Fifi Glusac? There are plenty of cross-eyed dames around; you could've got one who wasn't so tempertantrumental."

Bone ashed the cigar on the raven's forehead. "Desdemona, do you think I chose Fifi Glusac at random?"

"I dunno *where* you were when you chose her. Don't care either." She pecked a colony of fleas from her vent.

"La Stupido was not chosen because of her crossed eyes, she was chosen because of her physical talents. She is the only one I know who can accomplish what she can with just the human body as her equipment."

"Eh?"

"It was entirely beside the point that her eyes are how they are. But I *used* that little attribute of hers. Whenever I painted the Quetzal Queen's likeness, I recreated La Stupido's eyes. This is what I call *manipulating the world*. Geniuses such as what I am know how to turn things to our advantage, to make the world see the things we want it to see. Arrrrr."

"You're talking in circles. What do you mean, *her physical talents*?"

Bone swiped his arm across the chair, and Desdemona jumped down onto the limestone floor.

"Let me quote you a little something," he purred, lowering himself into the creaking chair. "Something I read in one of those books in the Mexico City Library, which, owing to my brilliant photographic-type memory—"

"Ha!" scoffed the bird.

"—I am able to repeat, word for word. Ahem:

The Elixir of Eternity is reputed to be kept by the Mayan Descendants of the Quetzal Queen in a place close to their ancient city. It is believed that the keeping place of the Elixir is at a location of great extremity, far removed from the obvious. Only the most nimble of body and mind will be able to locate and enter this secret location.

Did you hear that, raven? Only the most nimble of body and mind!"

"You? Nimble? You're about as nimble as a baby hippo in tights!"

"Arrr, don't cross me, you squabbling squidge of squirtiness, or I'll give you something that'll *really* make your stomach go yucky!"

"Nevermore, nevermore, nevermore!"

"I may not be the most nimble of men in body, but when it comes to the brain, none can surpass me. With my intellect and Fifi Glusac's physical prowess, we will be able to get my manicured fingers on that Elixir with no doubt about it."

"What's an extremity?" asked Desdemona, scratching her feathers.

"It's where I'd like to banish you, mollusc-breath. It's a place that is very hard to get to, a place that is almost impossible to reach. In my experience, extremities are often very high above the ground, like mountaintops or the peaks of glaciers or the uppermost heights of pyramids such as this one and all the others where I have painted the Quetzal Queen."

"Oh."

"And I have a feeling that when we have found this extremity, when the local natives have told us exactly where it is, there will only be a small space available for us to access it. Hence our reliance on La Stupido."

"Ah, now I get it ... she can squash herself up into one of those contortions she does, and squeeze into the extremity and grab the Elixir for us!"

"Precisely. Hence my recruitment of *this* woman instead of anyone else."

"Ha! The way she can tie herself up in knots, she's more like the *Pretzel* Queen than the *Quetzal* Queen. Get it?"

"*You'll* get it if you don't pipe down ... *Hello, what's that?*" Bone rose from his chair and stepped towards the top step of the staircase.

"What's what?" Desdemona hopped to the edge of the step and peered down into the thick dusk below, following Neptune Bone's gaze.

"Oh, look, see? They come! Arrrr."

Far below, at the edge of the perimeter of Chichén Itzá where the grass stopped and the trees began, a winking, shifting procession of tiny lights was appearing.

"The natives have come hither! Arrr, where is that wretched contortionist when you need her?"

Desdemona's eyes were cluttered with the sight. "Crark! There's hundreds of them, no, *thousands* of 'em! And they've all got a burning torch!"

"They've seen my light, Desdemona. As the world will, very very soon!" The large man moved closer to the edge of the top step, and took a huge sniff. "I have always believed that there is such a thing as what the poets call 'the sweet smell of success', and this is what I am smelling now…"

"You *are* smelling now, that's for sure," rasped Desdemona under her breath.

He watched the lights coming nearer, wafting closer towards the base of the Pyramid of Kukulcán. "They are such a long way below, they appear so small and inconsequential. Which, in my presence, is how it should be."

"Oh, brother," throbbed the raven.

Bone moved infinitesimally closer to the edge of the step.

Puffing out his chest, he filled his lungs with the sweet smell around him.

Opening wide his eyes, he filled his sights with the vision of the thousands of tiny lights approaching.

Flaring his nostrils broadly, he filled his beard with

a bristling of great anticipation – and moved forward just a tad.

And fell.

"*Arrrr*

    Arrrr

        Arrrr

            Arrrr

                Arrrr

                    Arrrr

                        Arrrr

                            Arrrr!"

There are ninety-one steep, steep steps on the northern staircase of the Pyramid of Kukulcán, and the substantial backside of Captain Neptune Flannelbottom Bone got to know every one of these steps very closely.

By the time he got to the bottom, with his waistcoat skew-whiff and his plus-fours trousers hitched uncomfortably up in the style of a Sumo wrestler's loincloth, he was a furious bundle of messiness …

… and the thousands of fireflies – they who had emerged from the bushes with their bright, tiny yellow lights glowing excitedly – found the sight of him repugnant, and flew back into the bush in a blaze of bewildered incandescence.

♚♚♚♚♚ **15** ♚♚♚♚♚

THE UNRAVELLING OF MEMORY

SINCE THE VISIT of Cairo Jim, Doris and Brenda to his dark and secret cabaña, Armando Tezzistecoátl's memory had revealed many things to the old man. Many things that he had not thought about for many, many years.

It was the mention of the Quetzal Queen that began this strange new flooding of memories. It was almost as if Jim had held a candle behind that part of Armando's brain where his memory was housed, and ever since, so many things that Armando's mother had once told him such a long time ago were now glowing again. And the more he thought about these glowing embers of the past, the stronger they became, until some of them were as bright as the day his mother had first told him.

He remembered lots of things now: how his parents had told him all about the moon and its great Mayan god who once looked down over all the earth below; how to stalk the iguana so it never knew you were there; how to make a sombrero that would last longer than anyone else's; how to avoid vacuum-cleaner sellers. But the brightest memories – those that took longer to light up, but when they *were* lit up,

they shone brighter than any others – were about the legend of the Quetzal Queen.

Armando was grateful that Cairo Jim had stumbled across him in the darkness that night, because now he was able to travel back to part of his past – part of his *yesterdays* – that he had not visited for many seasons.

Tonight the old man sat by the door of his cabaña, looking out at the falling darkness. His gramophone had wound down an hour ago, but he didn't get up to go and rewind it. He found that his newly lit memories were just as good company as the song he had heard so often in the past.

As the jungle began to swell with its night-time symphony of croaking, chattering, shrieking, crying, squelching and fluttering, another memory began to glow in the distant recesses of Armando's mind. Slowly he let the flame of Cairo Jim's candle move across it...

"Rark! How much further to this Uxmal place, Jim?"

"A few more hours, my dear." Jim reached forward to where Doris was perched on the front of Brenda's saddle, and gave the macaw's neck plumage a gentle tousle. "Don't worry, we'll get there."

"'I have watch'd and travell'd hard; some time I shall sleep out, the rest I'll whistle,'" quoted the bird.

"Very good, Doris."

"*King Lear* by Mr Shakespeare. Act Two, Scene Two. Rerark. Gosh I'm tired. I think I might just do as Mr S. suggested."

"Quaao!" Brenda snorted, her hoofs galloping steadily along the night-shrouded highway.

"You're doing wonderfully, Brenda my lovely," called Jim, patting the Wonder Camel's flank.

Her eyelashes trembled with pleasure as she continued her pace.

The archaeologist-poet straightened again in the saddle, and peered into the gloom ahead. It was an extremely dark night tonight, the darkest he could remember since they had arrived in Mexico. The only illumination they had had while they had journeyed eastwards from Palenque was from the headlamps of cars which overtook them every now and then, or came from the opposite direction.

But for the last couple of hours, as Brenda had travelled further and further into the wilderness, the roads had become much rougher, and there had not been many cars at all.

Jim began to drowse, his eyes growing heavy and his limbs becoming like bricks as he felt himself sinking deeper into the saddle. He raised high his eyebrows and his eyelids widened. He saw Doris teetering a little in front of him, and noticed that her head was cocked to the side, as it often was when she tucked her beak into her wing when she was sleeping. He smiled to himself and decided not to wake her; they would undoubtedly need all of their energy and astuteness for the search at Uxmal.

To try and keep *himself* awake, he began to think back to his time when he was at Archaeology School, studying ancient Mayan history. Maybe if he could recollect something from his studies about the Quetzal Queen, he might be able to remember where she kept the secret to her long life.

He thought and thought, casting his mind back to the days when he was a student. He could see the Archaeology School classroom with its small wooden desks and glass-doored cupboards full of dusty statues and small monuments; could picture himself sitting behind the neat and serious Millicent Spule who later made quite a name for herself in the study of early Hittite wigs and toupees; could almost hear again the voice of his favourite antiquities professor, Pasqual DeLirio; could even almost visualise the constantly empty seat of his fellow student, Neptune Bone, who was always off at the pyramids trying to sell tasteless plastic reproductions of ancient artworks – scarabs, ushabti figurines and nostril-hair clippers – to the gullible tourists.

But that was all; Jim couldn't recall *anything* about the Quetzal Queen of the Maya.

He shook his head and cast those memories back. Then, logically and carefully, he started to sort out all the things he knew for certain into a clear order in his mind:

1. Bone is after the secret to eternal life, that which the Quetzal Queen herself possessed. (This thought filled Cairo Jim's stomach with a mighty hollow dread, and caused his forehead to perspire freely.)

2. Bone had called this secret his "invaluable treasure", according to Armando.

3. Armando had told them that the Quetzal Queen reigned at her palace in Uxmal, where they were headed now.

4. Bone had kidnapped Mademoiselle Fifi Glusac.

5. Bone had painted the Quetzal Queen at a number of locations all across Mexico.

And there Jim stopped, for whatever else he knew was only conjecture. These were the only facts that he and Doris and Brenda had uncovered for sure.

The wind whistled past his pith helmet and spiralled all the hairs on his legs. Cairo Jim shut his eyes and hoped beyond all hoping that something more would be revealed when they got to Uxmal.

Armando was staring up at the stars when he heard his mother's voice.

"And," she said, her voice soft and gossamer-like, as though it were threading itself through the very fabric of time, "they called the Quetzal Queen's secret by a special name. It was a liquid which she drank every morning and evening, and which was brought to her by her maidens who waited on her royal person."

"Si?" Armando whispered to the sky. "Si? What did they call this liquid, Mother?"

"It was called the Elixir of Eternity."

Armando repeated the words. He had not heard his mother's voice for nearly eighty years.

"Si," his mother's voice said. "It was kept at a place of great extremity at the Pyramid of the Magician at Uxmal. Only the wise and the nimble could ever obtain it for the Queen."

"A place of great extremity?" whispered Armando.

A thin, silver covering of clouds filtered across the sky and the moon and the stars, and Armando's mother's voice was gone.

Distance is no threat, hindrance or obstacle to a Wonder Camel.

Not only can these noble and remarkable beasts cover great distances of land, they can also defeat the tyranny of *space*. Never more so than tonight was Brenda the Wonder Camel to appreciate this fact.

The moonlight was streaming through her hot mane as she thundered towards Uxmal; Doris was slumbering gently at the front of her saddle; Jim of Cairo was casting his mind back to his Archaeology School days, trying to dredge some facts up about the Quetzal Queen, when space, time and telepathy melded into a Wonder Camel concoction that reached her ears and entered her brain with a strange tingling.

From far away in Palenque, Armando's memory unravelled, and the words from it came forth:

"They called the Quetzal Queen's secret by a special name. It was a liquid which she drank every morning and evening, and which was brought to her by her maidens who waited on her royal person. It was the Elixir *of Eternity."*

"Quaaaooo!" Brenda gave a snort as the words settled in her brain. She was not surprised that they had come out of nowhere the way they did – this sort of thing had been happening to her ever since she was a small calf.

As she continued along the road, she received the rest of the message:

"*It was kept* at a place of great extremity *at the Pyramid of the Magician at Uxmal. Only the wise and the nimble could ever obtain it for the Queen...*"

"Quaaaoooo!" Brenda snorted again. She knew exactly what to do with this new knowledge.

Cairo Jim sat bolt upright. "Well swoggle me in the saddlebags!" he exclaimed loudly.

"Rerark!" Doris woke with a start at his voice. "What's up, Jim? You almost scared my claws off!"

"The memory is a marvellous thing," Jim said. "Do you know, I've been sitting here, trying to remember all I could about the Quetzal Queen from my days at Archaeology School, and not being able to come up with anything. Not a single fact, not an inkling of a recollection. And now, suddenly, I remember everything!" He pushed back the brim of his pith helmet and smiled a semi-astounded sort of smile.

"Like what?" flapped the macaw.

"Like the fact that the Quetzal Queen's secret was a liquid she drank every morning and night, and which was brought to her by the maidens who waited on her royal person. It was called the Elixir of Eternity, and it was kept at a place of great extremity at the Pyramid of the Magician at Uxmal. And only the wise and the nimble could ever obtain it for the Queen."

Doris hopped about to face him. "Are you sure about all this?"

Jim closed his eyes for a few seconds while he thought hard about her question. Then he opened them and answered. "Yes. I just felt it in my bones like you do when you're positive about something."

"Hmmm," Doris prerked. "The Elixir of Eternity, eh? A place of great extremity?"

"A place," nodded Jim, "that would've been very hard to get to. That only the wise and the nimble could reach."

"Well, between the three of us we've got a bit of wisdom and a good slab of nimbleness. Rark!"

"Now all we have to do is find exactly where this place of great extremity is," announced Jim urgently. "And hope we get to it before that overblown evil brute does."

"Rerk, step on it, Bren!"

"And hope," Jim said quietly to himself, "that we can find out exactly what he's up to."

"Quaaaooo!" snorted Brenda as she galloped along, pleased that she had played a small part in the proceedings.

'URTLING UNDER UXMAL

AS THEY APPROACHED the pathway leading to the great ancient site of Uxmal, Jim saw, through the moonlit gloom, the outline of a figure standing by the entrance gates to the site. It appeared to be the only figure around.

"Whoa, my lovely," Jim gently commanded. Brenda came to a smooth and puffing halt, her nostrils flaring broadly. With a gentle prod of his boot, Jim directed the Wonder Camel to walk towards the figure.

"Rark!" squawked Doris, seeing the figure for the first time.

The figure jumped at her squawk, and looked up at the group.

"Hello," said Jim.

"Are you with the Delegation?" asked the figure, who they could now see was a man dressed in shorts, a loose-fitting shirt and a felt hat. By his feet rested a small airline bag.

"Um, no," replied Jim. "My name's Cairo Jim. I'm an archaeologist, here on important business."

"Oh." The man looked bewildered, then extended his hand upwards. "I'm Bruce. Bruce Bellwether. From Bondi. I've lost my Delegation."

Jim shook his hand and let it go again. "What Delegation's that?"

"The International Vacuum-Cleaner Sales Delegation. We're here on a cultural tour of goodwill. But I seem to have lost them all, all seventy-two of my colleagues."

"Oh," said Jim.

"One minute we were all here together, wandering through the Nunnery Quadrangle over there behind the Pyramid of the Magician. I stopped to have a bit of a think about how hard it would've been to keep the walls in there dust-free in those ancient days, what with all of those criss-crossed carvings all over the place that represent snake scales – a mighty lot of dust particles can gather in all those nooks and crannies, believe you me, and all the Mayans would've had were *feathers* to do the dusting with, which of course would've been totally useless, as feathers can't *suck the dust out* – when I turned round, and my colleagues had all nicked off without me!"

"I'm sorry to hear that," Jim said.

"Rerk," Doris whispered urgently into Jim's ear, "let's go, Jim! Time is precious now!"

"And then," continued Bruce Bellwether, "I came out here to find the bus'd gone. I've been left here like a shag on a rock."

"Tell me," Jim enquired, "you haven't seen a man in there, have you? Very large, fleshy man, wearing a fez and an emerald-green waistcoat, probably smoking a foul cigar, and accompanied by a grotty raven and a very blonde, slightly cross-eyed woman?"

Bruce Bellwether scratched his sunburnt chin as he thought. "Nope," he frowned. "Can't say I have."

"Right," said Jim. "Mr Bellwether, I wish we could help you find your Delegation, but right now I'm afraid that's impossible. The whole survival of the free world, of a world that will continue to exist without eternal, monstrous tyranny and injustice, depends on our getting to the Pyramid of the Magician without delay."

"Yes," said Bruce Bellwether, picking up his airline bag. "It's usually the way, isn't it?" He smiled at them – a bewildered, lost sort of smile – and nodded. "Think I'll head up to the highway. See if I can hitch a lift back to Merida."

With a wave of his hand, he went off into the night.

"What an odd man," mused Jim, but Doris gave Brenda's neck a quick fluttering and urged her in no uncertain terms to get straight to the Pyramid of the Magician.

Doris sat on the crown of Jim's pith helmet, while he sat on Brenda's saddle. All three of them stared up at the immense, oval-based Pyramid of the Magician rising towards the midnight clouds. A little more than halfway up, there was a small dark opening in the staircase, a doorway fashioned in the shape of a serpent's mouth. Higher, at the top of the staircase, was the shadowy outline of a plain temple.

"So the Elixir is kept at a place of great extremity at the Pyramid, eh, Jim?"

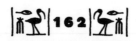

"As far as I remember, my dear."

"Quaaoo," Brenda snorted. "Let's try the temple at the top," she suggested telepathically.

"I reckon we should try looking in the temple at the top to start with," said Jim, reaching into Brenda's saddlebags and pulling out the three torches. "That seems like it might be the most extreme place attached to this pyramid. At least that's how it seems from down here."

"Mount those steps, then," urged Doris, taking her torch and screeching loudly into the night before flying up into the darkness.

This was definitely the toughest climb of all. The steps were narrower than any of the other pyramids or temples that Jim or Brenda had encountered so far; the sweep of the staircase soared upwards, onwards, as though it knew no bounds of space or time or reason.

The clouds above filtered what little light there was from the moon, creating a vague mist of moonshine that made the steps more deceptive, more shimmering, more *threatening* to Brenda's hoofs and Jim's hands and boots (for he had dismounted at the base of the Pyramid) than they actually were.

As Jim climbed higher, one hand above the other, one boot lifting to the next step and then the other boot to the one above it, his heart pounded heavily. "There's so little to go on," he kept thinking. "So much about all this that doesn't make sense. What if Bone actually *gets* his hands on the Elixir of Eternity? What if—?"

He stopped climbing; his heart was now pounding more fiercely than a can full of Mexican jumping beans. "What if Bone has *already got his hands onto it?*"

At that moment Brenda came up from below him and nuzzled the backs of his knees gently with her snout. "Quuuaaaaoooo," she snorted softly.

Jim took a deep breath. "You're right, my lovely. It's silly to anticipate what we don't yet know. Come on, up to the skies!"

Five minutes later, Doris greeted them at the top. "So nice of you to make it," she chirped, her wings on her hipfeathers. "If I'd known you were coming I'd've baked a cake!"

Jim sat, puffing heavily, on the top step and had a huge drink from his water-bottle. He could feel his heart batting against his ribcage and his kneecaps pounding from the inside. "How very nice of you, my dear," he breathed, putting the water-bottle back into Brenda's saddlebag.

"Quaaaooo!" Brenda was impatient to enter the temple.

"All right, Bren," screeched Doris, hopping up onto Jim's shoulder and blinking rapidly. "You lead the way this time."

The temple itself was a fairly plain, oblong structure, with a low roof that was only about a metre above Jim's head. Once, in its heyday, the temple would have been grand and imposing, with colourful reliefs painted on its walls inside and outside, and beautiful carved stone masks of the rain god, Chac, as well as countless criss-cross patterns representing snake scales adorning its surfaces. The plinth of the walls would have been decorated with small carved cylindrical drums, and all of it would have been bright and vivid.

Time, however, along with tourists' scuffing feet, had long since altered the temple. Now it was nothing more than a long, faded room, empty except for a few dozen small square slabs of rock scattered around the floor. And, of course, the painting of the Quetzal Queen which lay spread across it.

Jim looked down at the gaudy portrait. "If Bone had a day job, I'd advise him not to give it up too quickly," he commented, screwing up his nose.

"Well, where do we start looking?" Doris squawked. "Where do we find this place that only the wise and nimble could obtain the Elixir from?"

"Let's see," said Cairo Jim.

He placed his torch in one of the corners. Then he chose some of the solid, flattish rocks that were lying around, and pushed them across the rough floor to the torch. These he made into a platform, placing some of the smaller rocks on top of the heavier ones, at the front end of the small platform, the end furthest from the walls.

He picked up the torch, slid the small platform of rocks right into the corner so it was hard up against the walls, and rested the torch on the platform, so that the lamp end rested on the small rocks at the front. In this way the torchbeam was securely cast upwards at an angle, onto the opposite corner, where it lit a big part of the two walls there.

"Clever thinking, Jim," cooed Doris.

"I figure we're after some sort of secret panel or hidden passageway or something, maybe in one of these walls. If we can angle all our lights up from opposite corners, we should have enough illumination and light-spill to be able to view most of the surfaces in the temple. Then we can make a systematic, detailed examination, with our eyes, hands, wings and hoofs.

"A man of simple yet rare brilliance that lays all complication to the nonsense-pot," declaimed Doris.

"Very good, Doris. Shakespeare?"

"Rark, no. Doris. I just made it up." She did a small dance on the stones, happy with her inventiveness.

Stooping, Brenda took up Jim's initiative and with her snout began to nudge some hefty slabs of rock over to another corner.

"Thanks, my lovely. While you're moving those, I'll lug some more rocks over to this other corner for Doris's torch. Her wings are a little small for this job."

Doris stopped her dancing and blinked at him. "But my spirit is mighty."

"As no one would ever doubt," grunted Jim. He gave her an enormous smile as he pushed three squarish slabs across the Quetzal Queen painting – he enjoyed doing that – and towards the furthest corner.

Doris flew to the terrace outside the doorway and looked out, across the blackened forest and the other ancient buildings all shrouded in their night-time cloaks: the House of the Turtles, the Governor's Palace, the House of the Pigeons and the House of the Old Woman were only dim mounds of hulkingness tonight. "No sign of anyone down there," she announced, flexing up and down and opening her wings and folding them about her again. "No lanterns or lights or anything. Just darkness."

"Then at least we won't be disturbed," Jim murmured, putting the finishing touches to the small rock platform and setting Doris's torch upon it. Carefully he adjusted the angle, fiddling with it, trying to fix it until it was just right. As he squatted with his back turned to the rest of the temple, he was unaware of what was happening behind him:

A small sliding sound, a muffled slipping of hoofs on rock, and Brenda was gone!

⬥⬥⬥⬥⬥ 17 ⬥⬥⬥⬥⬥

SAY NO WHAT?

BEING CLOSER to the sounds, Doris *had* heard them.

She turned, her browfeathers furrowed. "Bren?" she cooed quietly to the empty corner where her Bactrian friend had been busy with her rocks.

Jim remained crouched and engrossed in his corner, still having trouble balancing the torch in exactly the position he was after – it kept rolling off to the side.

"Brenda?" Doris blinked. She waddled to Brenda's corner and poked her beak about the rocks. Not only had the Wonder Camel disappeared, but her torch had gone too.

"Hello?" whispered the macaw. She lifted her wings once and hop-fluttered up onto the top of the rock platform. Here she turned around and around, her eyes darting over the walls and the floor and the back of Cairo Jim, her tailfeathers brushing stiffly against the walls behind her as she turned.

A small sliding, the muffled scrape of claws on rock...

"There," muttered Jim, at last satisfied with the way the beam was being cast at Brenda's corner. Now there were two strong beams lighting most of the temple's interior. "We'll just fine-tune Brenda's, and Bob's your..."

He stood and turned.

"D ... Doris? B ... Brenda?"

And his words bounced back at him from the walls of the empty temple.

He waited a moment, then spoke again. "Come on out, you two. There'll be plenty of time for games, after we've squashed Bone's malevolent desires."

Silence.

"Tell you what, we'll even play that yawning game you're both so fond of."

He waited, but there was no answer.

"Doris, my dear? Brenda, my lovely?"

The only sound to be heard was a faint, moaning wind, curling and whistling around the upper portions of the Pyramid. "*Oooohhhhhhhhhhh – oooohhhhhhhhhhh...*"

"Well swoggle me solitarily," whispered Jim. He wiped his palms against his shirt front – they were perspiring heavily now – and looked all around him. There was clearly nowhere in that temple for a Wonder Camel and a macaw to be hiding.

Picking up Doris's torch, he went out the doorway and looked about the top terrace of the Pyramid. Nothing. With urgent steps he strode around the outside perimeter of the temple, coming back to where he had started. Nothing. His hand trembling, he shone the torchbeam down the gigantic staircase. Nothing.

A couple of large green moths, attracted by the light, flew about his head. He waved them away and went back inside the temple.

As he approached Brenda's corner, he saw that the pile of rocks she had been nudging and piling into her small platform hadn't been pushed right into the corner. They were positioned a little distance from the point where the two walls and the floor met.

Jim looked at the pile of rocks for some time, but his eye wasn't really concentrating on them; his thoughts and complete attention were focussed on the riddle of where his friends had gone. And how they'd gone there so swiftly and so quietly, without letting him know where they were going. It was most unlike them.

Lost in thought and worry like this, and without fully realising what he was doing, he pushed the pile of rocks with the tip of his left boot into the cranny of the corner. Just as Brenda had originally done with her snout, although Jim was not to know this.

The pile of rocks smacked into the stones on the rear and side walls, nestling against them in the cleft made by the two walls. Just in the exact spot where Doris's tailfeathers had come into fleeting but firm contact with the stones on those walls.

And a trigger was set off.

With barely a sound, the slabs of stone in the floor beneath Jim slid quickly away, so quickly that the archaeologist-poet found himself keeling over, for the briefest of moments half-standing, half-teetering on nothing but the empty space under his boots.

Then he fell onto his hands, and went sliding

headfirst down a ramp that was more slippery than any ramp he had ever encountered.

"*Whooooooooaaaaaaaaaaaaaa!*" he hollered as he plummeted downwards, into the dark void, while the floor of the temple above shot silently back into place, and Brenda's small platform of rocks moved away from the corner once again.

"*Heeeeeeeelllllppppppp!*"

Down, down, down he slithered, faster and faster, unable to control his sliding. He couldn't see a thing; the only smell that flew up his nostrils was that of dankness.

The further he plummeted, the moister his slide became. His shirt front and his shorts were soon soaking wet, and tiny droplets of liquid were spurting up and into his face.

Down,
  down,
  down,
  wetly down
    until he shot out of the ramp
    and into a great sea of blackness.

SPERLLLLLLAAAAAAAAAASSSSSSSHHHHH!

Cairo Jim plunged deep into the cool, dark water, his pith helmet shooting off as he hurtled downwards like a torpedo. He shut his eyes tightly, clamped his lips shut and quickly pinched his nostrils together, but not before getting a lungful and noseful of water.

For what seemed like minutes – long, bubbly minutes – he plunged deeper, until gradually his momentum started to slow. The water was almost icy-cold down here. He hadn't even hit the bottom when he found that he was able to kick against the water's depths and start to propel himself upwards again.

Up, up, up … his lungs were bursting for oxygen, but it was too soon for him to open his mouth just yet. He opened his eyes and saw, above him, a blurry light, faint and bobbing. On the other side of the water … on the dry side.

The higher he was rising, the less cold the water was getting.

With a huge pushing and kicking Jim surfaced, his head and shoulders bobbing about, out of the water, like a cork, the rest of his body still submerged.

He flung his mouth open, gasping for air, spluttering and splashing, and briefly went under again, getting another couple of huge gulps of water. Up he came, and this time, by treading water, he was able to keep himself afloat.

The small waves he'd created in his upping-and-downing lapped against his chin and into his gasping mouth.

He shook his head fiercely to get the water out of his hair and eyes and ears, and caught sight of the faint light ahead. Only now it was brighter, much brighter, and it seemed to be focussed on him.

Jim blinked at it, raised his hand timorously to shield his eyes from the full glare of it, and then, when he could see behind it, he smiled.

Enormously.

"Scrark!" screeched a drenched Doris, perched between the ears of a bobbing Brenda the Wonder Camel. "Welcome, buddy-boy!"

"Quaaaooo!" snorted Brenda, terrifically glad to see him once more. She had been hoofing water valiantly for some time now, with her torch in her mouth, and had been growing tired, but Jim's arrival gave her a new surge of buoyancy.

"My friends," Jim spluttered. "Reunited again. Thank Thoth!"

Doris flexed up and down and shook some of the water from her feathers. "Where are we, Jim?"

Still treading water, he looked around him.

They were deep in an underground cavern that was half-filled with a vast, seemingly bottomless and endless lake. High above, great pointy stalactites of green, crystallised rocks hung down from the cavern's roof. Some of the stalactites were as thick as the trunks of six trees; others were spindly, more like long, snaking twigs that were dangling in a frozen sort of limbo. A great number of the hugest stalactites had grown so long they were almost touching the water's surface.

As Brenda moved her torch this way and that, the light reflected off the stalactites in a million minuscule sparkles, and the entire cavern twinkled on and off, bright and dim, as if all the stars in all the galaxies had secretly come down here to show off to each other.

Cairo Jim began to laugh quietly – not only with

pleasure at the sheer beauty of it all, but largely with relief at having found his companions once more.

"Jim!" Doris squawked. "What *is* this place?"

"Cenote,*" breathed the archaeologist-poet. "Cenote."

"Note-ay," said Doris.

"What, my dear?"

"Note-ay." She bent low so her beak was close to Brenda's ear. "I think some water got into his brain. What sort of a word is 'note-ay'? And why does he want me to say it to him?"

"Quaaoo," shrugged Brenda, the water sloshing against her humps.

Doris straightened again. "Note-ay, note-ay, note-ay. There, I've said it!"

Jim looked puzzled.

"You told me," she explained patiently, "to say note-ay."

"Ah! No, Doris, we're *in* a cenote. It's the name for an ancient Mayan well such as this, far beneath the earth. These cenotes were extremely important to the Maya … the waters usually come from massive underground rivers or springs. Sometimes we don't know *where* they originate from. Often, in ancient times, the civilisations depended entirely on cenotes for their water supplies, especially if there were long periods of drought, which happened quite often around these parts."

---

* Pronounced say-NOTE-ay.

"Coo," cooed the macaw.

"Quaaaooo."

"That's part of the reason why these wells were considered to be sacred." Jim cupped his hand and scooped some of the water to his lips. He took a long, slow sip of it. "I've never known water to taste so sweet, not in all my days. It's so ... so *pure* ... and sweet, like a trillion drops of bees' nectar. Yet it's not sticky or coloured or anything. Look at how *clear* it is."

"We've found that out already," prerked Doris. "We both got bellyfuls of it when we came sliding down. You weren't the only one to make a splash-landing, you know!"

Jim sipped some more of the pure water.

"What worries me," Doris went on, "is how do we get out? We can't stay here treading and hoofing water for ever. Brenda'll be growing *fins* before long."

Brenda saw something then. "Quaaaoooo!"

"What is it, my lovely?"

The Wonder Camel shone her torchlight off into a distant, dark grotto that lay between four extremely large and long stalactites. The minerals in the stalactites glinted like tiny, winking neon lights.

"Look, Doris, she's found something."

"Listen," implored Brenda with a special snort.

"Listen," Doris whispered. "There's a noise coming from in there."

They fell silent, and gradually they heard it: a faint moaning that sounded as if it were being pulled and stretched upwards and away from them. That sounded as though it was being drawn across the rack of Time itself.

Aaaaaaaaaaaahhhhhhhhhh...

"It's wind," Jim said. "It's a wind current, being sucked up and out. Come on, let's swim closer."

Slowly they did so, Jim taking in a few deliberate swallows of the beautiful, refreshing water as they paddled towards the grotto. On the way he collected his floating pith helmet and plonked it wetly onto his head.

When they were close to the grotto Brenda shone her torch deep within.

"Rark! Look, it's an opening!"

"A shaft," declared Cairo Jim. "Going up, at an angle. Small, but not too small for a macaw, an archae-ologist, and a Wonder Camel who can self-deflate her humps for small periods of time, to pass through. Brenda, you clever thing!"

"Good one, Bren!"

"Quaaaooo." There was a modest fluttering of eye-lashes.

"Now here's what we'll do," announced Jim, taking charge. "Doris, I'll give you the longest rope we've got in the saddlebags. You fly upwards, all the way to the surface, if the shaft goes that far, and tie the end of the rope around something permanent and substantial. Something very large. Then I'll carefully..."

♠♠♠♠♠ 18 ♠♠♠♠♠

ARRIVAL OF A QUEEN

THE BUGATTI PURRED SLEEKLY into the grounds of Uxmal, and came to a shuddering halt before the Pyramid of the Magician.

"Right," sneered Neptune Bone, turning off the engine and throwing open the driver's door. "Everybody OUT!" With an effort he managed to squeeze his bulky body out of the small doorway.

"Crark!" Desdemona's eyeballs throbbed redly as she leaned against the windscreen and clutched at her belly. "Oooh, I think my collywobbles have had babies. Must've been that spicy frajita I stole from that lady when we stopped to get petrol. Yergh!"

"I'll give you collywobbles, you greedy growth of gruesomeness. Control your inner unsteadiness, lest you destroy this, my night of greatest triumph yet!"

"Ha!" scoffed Fifi Glusac, sitting in a tangled sort of way in the back seat of the car, and fully attired as the Quetzal Queen, with her artificial feathered headdress on her head and the clip-on green plastic ornaments stuck to her earlobes and the underside of her nose.

She put down her harmonica (she had been playing a sad rendition of 'Pop Goes the Weasel' all the way

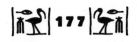

from Chichén Itzá) and glared at him. "What are you babbling about, your 'night of greatest triumph'? Ze only zing zat you are a triumph at is being a great big blob of a failure!"

Bone spun around like an overweight jaguar, and fixed her with a hostile glare. "Mademoiselle Glusac—"

"La Stupenda, M'sieur Zoomah!"

"Mademoiselle Glusac, hold your tongue! Or better yet, contort it into a knot so that I do not have to listen to your monumental stupidity!"

"Heh heh heh," sniggered Desdemona, pecking at a flea on her wing.

"Remember, madam, we are *both* very close to obtaining our separate *invaluable treasures*." He took off his fez and went to the travelling trunk next to Fifi. Opening it quickly, he threw the fez inside and withdrew another one – a chocolate-brown model with a Turkish-delight-coloured tassel. This he shoved onto his greasy hair. "Arrr. That's better," he said, now slightly less hysterical. "It's amazing how calming an item of stylish fashion can be."

"Ah!" Fifi sneered. "'Ow can you be so certain zat zis is ze night when we will get what we want? Every ozzer night 'as been nozzing but a disaster."

Bone slowly rubbed his fingers along his plaid-covered, bruised bottom (there was much of it, and he was rubbing for some minutes). "I am well aware that the preceding nights have not been what you would call a whale of a success," he spoke.

"Crark, they weren't even a *tadpole* of a success," crowed Desdemona.

"Shut your beak! I *am* aware that things haven't gone entirely to plan, and I have the bruises to it."

Fifi's eyes widened as she watched him rubbing his backside. "Well, don't show me!" she shrieked loudly. "Zat is *one* sight I 'ave no desire to lay my eyes on!"

"It'd be *two* sights, actually," Desdemona rasped. "Two very large ones."

"*I said shut it!*" Bone reached over, picked up the bird by her throat, and flung her far into the night. Her wings flapped wildly as she disappeared into the blackness.

"'Ey, you be careful wiz 'er! Remember, Zoomah, zose feathers are mine at ze end of all of zis!"

"I haven't forgotten, madam. And have them you shall, very soon I think." A smile of creeping anticipation spread across his fleshy lips.

"You seem very sure of yourself."

"And why shouldn't I be? Answer me that. When you think about it, Fifi old babe, this is the night of greatness. It has to be. All of the other possibilities for success have gradually been eliminated. Arrrr."

"I don't understand." Fifi shifted in the seat, getting herself into a more comfortable position – more comfortable for her at least: she hooked her feet together and brought both legs up and over her headdress so that her ankles were behind her neck.

"Explain 'ow you come to *zat* conclusion," she said, folding her arms in front of her.

"Because of the mere fact that this is the last of the important ancient Mayan sites where the Quetzal Queen could have dwelled. It was probably around here somewhere that I was camped that wonderful night when I tripped in the undergrowth and found those glyphs that told me all about her."

"I see."

Bone's smile broadened as he reached into the car and pulled out his long pole with the flammable rags tied to the top. "Arrr, this *has* to be the place! All of those other sites were merely test-runs for what is about to happen here tonight. Little *rehearsals*, you might call them. Being from the entertainment world, from the world of the *pretend*, I'm sure you understand the importance of *rehearsals*, don't you, *Fi*?"

"La Stupenda!"

He took his silver cigar-lighter from the pocket of his emerald-green waistcoat. "Without rehearsals, things couldn't go right, could they? Now, because you have rehearsed a few times, you are used to your Quetzal Queen costume. You no longer trip on that smock, nor do you get your headdress caught up in low-hanging tree branches. And I doubt very much that you'll get your nose ornament stuck up your right nostril again, like you did at Chichén Itzá."

"Zat was ze most painful zing I can remember," she squirmed. "It was even worse zan ze time I got cramps in all my toes when I was doing ze splits in Mombasa while I was playing 'Song of ze Volga Boatman'."

"Now you know how to play the part! Arrrr!"

"Tell me, m'sieur, what will you do when you 'ave got your 'ands on zese rubies you are after?"

"Rubies? What ru ... oh, yes, the *rubies*. Why, madam, let's just say that I shall enjoy them for longer than you could ever imagine. Ha ha ha ha ha ha ha ha haaarrrrrr!"

Desdemona circled above them, looking warily down at the laughing, wobbling figure of Bone. "Well," she thought, "he seems to be enjoying himself. Maybe it's safe to go back." She stilled her wings and dived quietly down, to land on the bonnet of the car, a safe distance from Bone.

He heard her talons screeching on the metal as she landed. "Hello, there, petite Dessie," he smirked.

"Crark. Are you over your little bout of hurlingness?" she croaked warily.

"Mm? Oh, heavens to the goddess Betsy, yes. Please forgive me and come closer." He wiggled his eyebrows in a come-hither fashion.

Warily she inched towards him. "Why, my Captain?"

"Why?" He smiled sweetly and flabbily.

"Why?" repeated Desdemona.

"*This is why!*" With one deft movement he performed three acts: he grabbed her by the throat, pulled her close, and quickly bound the long pole to her head by wrapping a rope that was threaded through a hole in the lower end of the pole tightly around her underbeak and the top of her skull.

"Bleeeeerrrrkkkk!" bleeeeerrrrkkkked the raven, finding it hard to fully open her beak now.

He tied the rope into a hard knot, so the long pole stood straight up from the top of her head, like an over-sized matchstick, and he raised his cigar-lighter to the top and flicked open the cover. In an instant the top of the pole – the rags and waddings – burst aflame.

"Aaaaarrrkkk!" wailed Desdemona.

"'Ey!" protested Fifi. "Don't you singe zose feathers!"

"Now, you lit-up litany of lunacy, get up onto the Pyramid steps and start hopping about. Flutter if the inclination so takes you. But keep moving. I want the natives out there – and I'm sure they *are* out there – to see my light!"

Fifi spoke up again, but this time her voice was barely more than an excited whisper: "I don't zink she'll need to do *zat*, M'sieur Zoomah."

"What?" Bone glowered down at the contortionist from beneath his caterpillarian eyebrows. "Why ever not?"

"Because I zink ze natives know we are 'ere. Look!" She pointed out into the darkness with her left foot.

Sure enough, through the silhouetted trees and leafiness of the surrounding bush of Uxmal, thousands of huge flames were coming towards them, weaving in and out, disappearing behind black branches and blurry clusters of foliage. But definitely coming closer.

"Madam," Bone hissed, "lower your legs, if you

please! Royal Persons are never seen with their feet above their head!"

"Depends on ze guillotine," Fifi thought. She lowered her legs and adopted a dignified position more suitable to the Quetzal Queen.

"They're coming closer," stated Desdemona obviously.

"I can see that, you feathered numbskull. Keep hopping about, keep moving, while I help the Quetzal Queen to emerge from the automobile here."

"Ooh la la," gasped Fifi as Bone yanked her by the arm in his attempts to help the Quetzal Queen to emerge from the automobile. "Look at all zose flames. Zere must be 'undreds of zem!"

"More like thousands," grunted Bone. "Let's hope they're all not the flames of silly old men in their night-gowns, or repellent insects with an Edison complex, trying to be airborne lightbulbs."

"Crark, no, they're … they're humans!"

"'Umans?" said Fifi, standing on the ground now and straightening down her smock and fiddling with her headdress.

"Arrrr, you're right, bird. From their outline they do appear to be human."

Fifi's crossed eyes were wide. "Well, glaze moi and bake moi and call moi a croissant! Look, zey are all so *tall*!"

All around Bone, Desdemona and Fifi, the bushes were parting, and a vast wall of tall, slender figures was slowly, *silently* advancing, closing in on the trio like a sea of water around a small island. Three thousand torches blazed above, brighter than the desert sun in the middle of the day.

"They *are* tall," gasped Bone, his eyes lit up by the flames. "Why, each of 'em must be over two and a half metres high!"

Desdemona's eyes throbbed the colour of a glowing sunset. "Blecchhh!" she spat as the sea of figures moved closer. "They're all *women*!"

"So zey are."

"Go tell it on the mountain," Bone said quietly to himself. "How extraordinary!"

Each of the women was dressed in a simple, ochre-coloured tunic that extended from her neck down to her knees. Each of them had six long blue feathers inter-twined through her long, dark, waist-length hair. These feathers hung down as though they were actual strands of the hair itself.

"Arrr, see those feathers! I knew this was the place!"

Now that the women were moving very close to Bone, Fifi and Desdemona, something else about the throng became visible under the bright flames: each and every one of the very tall women was carrying a long, long spear. Every spear was exactly the same height as the woman carrying it.

By this time, the women had formed themselves into a perfect circle, fifty women deep, around the trio. They stopped in their tracks, and stared at the intruders without so much as a whisper.

Bone looked all around the circle.

Fifi looked at Bone.

Desdemona looked ridiculous.

The only sound in the night was the loud crackling from the three thousand flames of the women and the one burning torch of the raven.

Large beads of sweat began to plop out of Bone's forehead and run down into his beard and moustache – it was getting devilishly hot being surrounded by all that fire.

Then Fifi hissed out of the side of her mouth: "Well, you 'uge fortune-'unter, what are you waiting for? You 'ave your audience! Get ze show on ze road!"

"Shut it, madam, and get ready to give the performance of your life." He nervously scanned the women, trying to find one who looked vaguely in charge. "Er, ahem. Good evening, ladies and … ladies. Do you have a leader by any chance?"

The women looked down on him and his friends, but remained as silent as stones.

"Arr, is there anyone with whom maybe I could speak?"

The silent staring continued.

Desdemona clutched at her stomach. "Oooh, I think I'm going to do something regrettable."

Bone sighed loudly. "Oh, for pity's sake, I think all the lights are on but nobody's at home!"

"We *are* at home," came a loud voice, soaring out

from the throng like a mighty wave. "Which is more than I think *you* are."

"Ooh," oohed Desdemona, forgetting about her stomach for the moment. "They speak."

Three thousand women parted – fifteen hundred to one side and fifteen hundred to the other – and there emerged into the circular clearing the tallest, most slender woman yet.

The women joined ranks again, behind the tallest woman, and the circle was once again complete.

This woman was nearly three metres tall. Unlike the other women, she carried no flaming torch or spear, and threaded through her hair were not six feathers, but *one* bright blue feather. It was the most lustrous of all the feathers that were on display.

She raised a long, strong, slender arm, and held it horizontally so that her fingers were pointed at Bone. "My name is Lupé," she told him, her voice softer now, but still surging with such command that Bone could feel the hairs on the backs of his hairs standing to attention. "I bring these people here. What brings you?"

"*My moment has at last arrived,*" thought Bone, his sense of grandeur rippling throughout his enormous body like a small tidal wave. A wide smile of power bloated his lips, and he removed his fez from off his head in a pretend act of homage.

"What brings me here is the most wonderful thing to happen to your people and your history, Lupé, since time began." He reached out and took the hand of

Fifi Glusac. "Behold! Tonight I, a humble and modest servant of the mysteries of the entire world, give you your past." He took a deep breath, his beard bristling, his eyes filling with pretend tears, and spoke:

"Ladies and ladies, it is my great pleasure to be able to present to you, for the first time and sparing no expense or trouble, she who lives eternal! BEHOLD YOUR QUETZAL QUEEN!"

Fifi looked nervously around and then bowed her head timidly.

For a full minute there was silence.

And then came laughter.

Thousands of mouths opened wide; thousands of heads were thrown back; peals of derisive giggling and cackling and wide-open howling erupted into the night air. The noise was so loud it could have shifted the course of the clouds overhead.

Desdemona slapped her wings over her hearing-holes to try and blot out the din. "Was it something you said?" she shouted at Bone.

"Arrr," he wobbled uncertainly.

Fifi straightened again and glared at him. "Never 'ave I 'ad *zis* kind of reception."

Lupé's arm shot straight up above her head. Instantly the women stopped their laughter.

"You are lying to us," Lupé accused.

"No, no, no, I assure you I am not. This" – he grabbed Fifi's hand and pulled her forward – "is your great Quetzal Queen. She who reigned over your ancestors many hundreds of years ago. She who reigned for nearly *eight hundred years*. And she who *will* reign over you all again, for many millennia to come!"

"'Ey," hissed Fifi, "wait just a minute, Zoomah! If you zink I am going to stay 'ere wiz all zese giantesses for even anozzer *day*, you've got anozzer zink coming!"

"Shh, madam, let me continue, and all will be well." He took a step towards Lupé. "I have brought her back to you. I have reunited all of your yesterdays with your todays. I am giving you your greatness again."

He looked up at Lupé, and she down at him.

"Of course I have done this out of the goodness of my generous and big heart," Bone smiled. "Without any wish for reward or praise. But the Queen is tired after her long journey ... we have come a long, long way, you see ... and so it is of great importance that she is able to be waited on immediately. What she needs, Lupé, is her" – and his voice dropped to a whisper so that Fifi couldn't hear him – "*Elixir of Eternity!*"

"Wicked liar!" Lupé brought her arm swiftly down, slicing through the air.

In a blink of time, the women at the front of the circle surged forward and swished their spears downwards, so that the pointed tips – sharper than razor blades, and fifty times bigger – were aimed at Bone, Fifi and Desdemona.

"I wish I were in Cairo wiz Gerald Perry Esquire," Fifi moaned, putting her head in her hands. "Even if 'e *does* suck 'is dentures!"

"Aarrgghh!" screamed Bone, staring at the hundred glinting speartips that would soon transform him into an overblown pincushion. "I'm too great to die…"

"Crarararrrk, you great big fool," throbbed Desdemona. She flapped her wings, but it was no good; the weight of the lit pole on her head prevented her from taking off. "You've really landed us in it this time!"

Lupé stepped to one side and gave a slow nod of her head.

The circle moved inwards.

The spears moved closer and closer, until the points were pressed against Bone's belly, Desdemona's wings and Fifi's tanglier bits.

Lupé fixed Bone with a look of deep scorn, and was just about to order that Bone, Desdemona and Fifi be thoroughly ventilated, when there was a loud commotion from behind, coming from the edge of the staircase of the Pyramid of the Magician.

And all the women stopped.

19

BONE MOVES QUICKLY

THE SHAFT LEADING UP from the deep bowels of the sacred cenote had been very tight and narrow. For Doris, this had been no problem: with the rope in her beak, she had corkscrew-flown to the top, where she had discovered that the shaft opened out onto the above-ground world at a spot at the base of the grand staircase of the Pyramid of the Magician.

Here, unaware of the confrontation that was happening a little distance away, she had tied her rope around the beak of one of two great carved quetzals that was guarding the stairs.

For Jim, the climb up the shaft hadn't been much of a problem either. He had managed to squeeze himself up without grazing his arms or legs or knuckles. Soon he was at the top also, and he and Doris were lying across the steps, reaching down into the shaft, and whispering words of encouragement to Brenda, who was doing her Bactrian best to hitch herself up the rope.

For Brenda, it *was* a problem getting up that shaft. She was doing all right until about halfway up, when she began to feel the rough sides closing in on her. *The shaft was getting narrower.* There was only one thing

for it – she decided to deflate her humps, as Jim had suggested earlier.

She had sucked in all of the breath she could and, with a tiny sighing sound, her humps had gone down, like balloons at the end of a very long party. This had helped her move higher for another couple of metres, but that was all. The walls of the shaft were still too narrow for her.

For a few long and sweaty minutes she had remained wedged inside the shaft, trying to inch herself upwards at first, and then downwards. But she wasn't budging. She was stuck fast.

"Quuuaaaaaoooo?" she snorted quietly, looking up to where Cairo Jim was shining his torchlight down at her.

"Brenda! Come on, push!"

Then the winds rose.

Far below, at the bottom, faint swirlings of breeze gathered and started to travel up the shaft. These faint swirlings grew stronger as they rose higher, and more swirlings joined them from the bottom of the cenote, growing stronger also. Upwards they sped, increasing in blowingness, and the narrowness of the shaft made the swirls of wind stronger and stronger.

The shaft was in fact a natural wind-tunnel, and by the time the fast-moving wind currents had reached Brenda's tail, they had all the strength of a minor tornado.

Suddenly Brenda had felt her tail and her hind

quarters being blasted by the gale. In the next second, she found herself whizzing up, up and up, the wind getting between her sides and the sides of the shaft wall and acting as a natural buffer between rock and Wonder Camel.

Wwwwhhhhhhhooooooooooosssssssssshhhhhhhh!

"Quuuuuuuuuuuaaaaaaaaaaaaooooooooooo!"

Up, up, up, up, up, until at last she reached the opening. With an enormous *POP* she erupted from the shaft and flew high into the air.

Jim and Doris pulled their heads and beaks away just in time to watch her shooting over.

Brenda fell to the ground, still buffeted by the breezes which – now they had reached the surface – had calmed down slightly. But they were still forceful enough to give the Wonder Camel a cushioned landing on the soft grass, although with a bit of a thud. Screeching and shouting, Doris and Jim had leapt from the staircase and rushed to see if she was all right.

This was the commotion that had stopped all the tall, slender women in their pointy tracks.

The sea of women opened a little (the ones at the front still keeping their spearpoints in firm, pressing contact with Bone, Desdemona and Fifi), and Lupé rushed towards Jim, Doris and Brenda.

Under all the flame-light Bone saw them also, and he thought fast:

"Madam, madam," he cried. "I am not wicked, nor am I a liar, you must believe me. No, *they* are the wicked ones!" He flung a pudgy finger in the direction of Jim, Doris and Brenda. "*They* have come here to steal the invaluable treasure of your tribe – the Elixir of Eternity itself! I was merely asking for it to keep it from them. This is why I am here, to stop them, to thwart their wicked ways, to save your ancient people from—"

"Bone!" Jim shouted. "You lying scum!"

"Bone?" said Fifi. "'Oo is zis *Bone*?"

Bone moved several of the spearpoints away from his waistcoat with the tips of his index fingers. "Madam," he quickly addressed Lupé, "do not listen to this man. He is well-known throughout the world as a swindler and gross extortionist. He is as deceitful as the night is long! His underhandedness is legendary!"

Lupé looked at Jim, then at Bone, then at Jim again.

"He is here," Bone continued, his voice getting higher, "to try and steal your heritage! See, he has brought his accomplices with him – the bird and the humped monstrosity!"

Lupé approached Cairo Jim. "Is what he is saying the truth?" she asked, looking down on him and Doris and Brenda.

Jim quickly removed his pith helmet. "No, absolutely not. My name is Jim, Jim of Cairo, and my friends and I are here to try and protect you from—"

Bone yelled out, "He even defaced your beautiful temple high atop the Pyramid with that painting!"

Lupé's eyes blazed angrily. "So that was *you*?" she seethed at Cairo Jim.

"Rarrrrrk!" screeched Doris.

"Quuuuuaaaaaoooo!" squeal-snorted Brenda.

"Absolutely not," answered Jim.

"Absolutely *was*," shouted Bone. "I saw him do it!" With a swift plunging movement, Bone's hand disappeared into his plus-fours trousers, and pulled out an antique miniature blunderbuss gun. "Allow me the honour, madam, of finishing them all off!"

Fifi Glusac swooned in a dead faint.

"At last, at last, at last," throbbed the raven. "Get those gaudy macaw feathers for me, Captain!"

Before Lupé could respond, Bone shoved his fez on his head, extended his arm and pointed the weapon directly at the heart of Cairo Jim. "You first, you under-handed heroic hokeyness," he growled. His finger tightened around the trigger. "You remember the Old Relics Society's motto, don't you, Jim? 'Old Relics Get Older By the Minute, And So Do You.' Well," he pointed to his overblown chest with his free hand, "not *this* pinnacle of brilliance. Arrrrr!"

Bone brought the miniature blunderbuss level with his eye and squinted while he kept the gun trained on Jim's heart. His pudgy finger curled closer round the trigger ...

... and froze.

"Crark! Go on, go on, go on," Desdemona crowed. "What're you waiting for?"

Bone's eyebrows bristled. One by one, the hairs in them – and there was a jungle of hairs in them –

stood on end. "Listen!" he whispered sibilantly. "Can you hear it?"

The raven cocked her head. "Hear what?"

"Put it down, Bone," cried Jim. "Before you—"

"SHUT UP!" Bone kept the gun extended at Jim, while looking up through his stiffened eyebrows. "That noise again … listen, it's getting closer!"

Desdemona rolled her eyeballs. "I don't hear anything, except the fleas munching in my feathers."

"I tell you it's up there, it's coming closer, it's—"

There was an enormous *flump-flump-flumping* from behind the Pyramid of the Magician. As though in a whirlwind, the nearby trees parted wildly and through them, down onto the ground, swooped the colossal Sphinx of the Naxians!

"Craaaarrrrrk!" wailed Desdemona, "it's that wretched statue you brought to life when we were in Greece! The Big Wings are back!"

The women on the eastern side of the circle – the side closest to this horrendous creature – quickly moved away a safer distance. Only Lupé stood her ground.

The Sphinx sat there, its gigantic curved wings opening above its head – the head of a human woman – and closing down by its side again. Its lean lion's body rippled with muscles and its strong claws scratched through the dirt as it pawed the ground. Then it became still – perfectly still, except for its tail which continued to swish against its flanks, up and down like a slow-motion whip.

Captain Neptune Flannelbottom Bone was sweating from every pore of his hide. His clothes were drenched, and his fez slipped off his head. Hoping to strike first, he moved his arm steadily away from Cairo Jim, and towards the female head of the Sphinx.

"Don't look this way, you leonine lump of marble," he murmured so quietly to himself that the sound of his words was drowned out by the echoing beating of his heart.

The blunderbuss was pointing directly at the Sphinx's head. Bone scrunched his eyes to try to get the dribbling beads of sweat out of them, opened them again, and was just about to pull the trigger when ...

... the mighty Sphinx pounced through the air, its talons sprung, and closed its huge paws around Bone's left leg.

"*Ouuuuuuccchhhh! No, no, no!*" shrieked the terrified man, dropping the blunderbuss as the creature flexed its wings and rose slowly into the air. "Watch those claws! Have mercy, please! I was only fulfilling a destiny whose only crime was being full of ambition ... where's the harm in ... *Heeeeeeeelllllllpp! Mother, heeeeeeeeeeeeeeeeeeelllllllllppppp!*"

But already his cries were fading away as the Sphinx took off over the night-shrouded bushland.

"Hey, wait for me!" wailed Desdemona, her eyes throbbing desperately. She tore away the rope from her underbeak, the lit pole falling to the ground.

"Without him, I'm nothing! Give him *baaaaaaaaaccccccc-cccckkkkkkkkk*!"

Soon she, too, was nothing more than a bad smell.

"Just as I've always thought," Jim said quietly to Doris and Brenda. "Your past always catches up with you at some stage or another."

"What an ugly creature," Doris scowled.

"She's a sight, isn't she?"

"Not the Sphinx of the Naxians," Doris said. "I meant Neptune Bone."

Lupé came close to them now and spoke gravely. "I do not understand what has gone on here," she said. "There is a lot of explaining you must do."

"I'll be glad to," Jim offered.

"But not to me. Not to us. There is someone very special you must appear before. Only then will all explanations be heard."

20

THE WISE AND THE NIMBLE

"AND THIS IS WHAT you know?" asked the young woman reclining on the bench.

"As much as I am certain of," answered Jim, standing before her and nervously fingering his pith helmet.

Lupé and a band of the tall, slender women had led Jim, Doris, Brenda and Fifi through a long, underground passageway built of Mayan arches, behind the Pyramid of the Magician. This passageway had brought them into a huge, beautifully decorated room, with a gleaming tiled floor and, at the far end, an enormous, jaguar-shaped bench covered with many plump and soft-looking cushions. It was on this bench, amidst all the cushions, that the young woman was lying.

"And this man Bone," the woman went on. "What relation is he to you, mademoiselle?"

Fifi rolled her eyes (she had been divested of her artificial headdress and ornaments before they had entered the passageway). "'E is no relation to me, I can assure you. I zought 'is name was Montgomery Zoomah until *zis* good man turned up." She looked at Jim thankfully. "I can give you my word zat what Cairo

Jim 'as told you is as true as I am aware. Why, I 'ad 'ardly any idea what Bone was up to. 'E told me 'e was after *rubies*."

"No," said the woman, who was dressed in a long, velvety leopard-skin gown. "There are no rubies here. He was after something far more unattainable than rubies."

"He was after the *legend*, perhaps?" ventured Doris.

The woman smiled, as did Lupé, who was standing a little way from the jaguar-shaped bench. "You are a wise bird," the woman said.

"Thank you," Doris blushed.

"Yes," Jim said. "It seems that Bone had read up on the legend, all right. I remember from my days at archaeology school, when we studied the Quetzal Queen—"

"Quaaooo," Brenda snorted knowingly.

"—that it was said that the Elixir of Eternity was kept at a place of great extremity at the Pyramid of the Magician. Only the wise and the nimble could ever obtain it for the Queen."

"Is that so?" said the woman.

"And that's probably why," Jim continued, "he kidnapped Mademoiselle Glusac here. You see, she's the most famous simultaneous harmonica player and contortionist in the world – she can tie herself up into all sorts of strange knots without losing her tune – and Bone was hoping that when he found this place of great extremity, Mademoiselle Glusac could squeeze or bend or slip herself into it, to get the Elixir."

"Ze crafty devil!"

"I see," nodded the woman. "And that explains why the dreadful painting appeared in the temple."

"Yes," Jim agreed. "He set the whole thing up. If he could produce a flesh-and-blood version of the painting, he thought that he could truly convince those who believed the legend of the Quetzal Queen that their *real* Queen had returned."

The woman sat up and leaned forward, resting her elbows on her knees. For several long minutes she gazed deep into the eyes of Cairo Jim, and saw the honesty within the man.

"Excuse me," Jim said at last, a little uncomfortable at having such a beautiful woman gazing intensely into his eyes for so long.

"Yes, Cairo Jim?"

"I was wondering if I might ask you a small question?"

"You may," smiled the woman. "And I shall see if I can give you a small answer."

Jim smiled back. "Well, you know who *we* all are, and I was wondering … *who are you*? And what is this ornate and lavish place?" He looked around the walls, at all of the vibrant woven tapestries that covered nearly every square centimetre, and at the high clay pots and vessels that stood in all of the corners by the archways.

The woman looked at Lupé. "I think we should answer that for our visitors, don't you, Lupé?"

"If it is your desire," Lupé replied.

The woman came down from the plushly cushioned, jaguar-shaped bench. She stood – in all her tall glory – before the gathering, and Lupé went through a tapestry-covered doorway behind the bench. She soon returned, carrying in her arms a shimmering green-blue bundle. This she raised to the head of the woman, and with great care, set it down.

"Ooh la la," gasped Fifi. "What an 'eaddress! It is so beautiful!"

"Cooo," coooed Doris, admiring the feathers that fell down past the woman's waist, and feeling pride in her *own* feathers.

"Quuaaaooo," snorted Brenda, her nostrils quivering excitedly.

"Well swoggle me stunningly." Jim brought his hand to his mouth.

The woman in the magnificent headdress smiled, serenely and warmly.

Lupé smiled also. "Behold the mighty Quetzal Queen," she announced. "Welcome to her Palace."

Jim knelt then, as did Fifi (wrapping one leg under her opposite arm at the same time) and Brenda, going down on her front legs first. Doris gave a long and respectful bow of her beak.

"Stand, please," said the Quetzal Queen.

They did so.

"So," Jim stammered, hardly able to think straight, "it's not all legend? You *are* real?"

"I am as real as the plants that grow, and the waters

that run." The Queen smiled. "I am satisfied with what you have told me, Cairo Jim. But now you all must leave us. My people do not encourage visitors; we have found that to be a threat to our existence. I made one mistake about five hundred years ago, with a Spanish conquistador named Cortés. He almost destroyed us all. I can't afford to take any more chances like that one."

"I understand," Jim said.

"Go now, and do not tell of my existence or our whereabouts." She stepped closer to him, gazed deeply into his eyes again, and saw his integrity reflected like clouds in a pool of still water. "I know I can trust you."

"Thank you," said Cairo Jim. "You certainly can."

"Prerark," prerarked Doris. "Adiós, oh Quetzal Queen."

"Adiós, Doris. Adiós, Brenda, you noble creature."

"Quaaaooo." Brenda fluttered her eyelashes nobly.

"Au revoir, your majesty," farewelled Fifi.

Two tall woman led them to the grandest doorway. By the colossal Mayan arch above this doorway, Jim turned. "Great Quetzal Queen," he ventured. "The Elixir of Eternity. It still exists, obviously. Where—?"

"Adiós, Jim of Cairo." The Quetzal Queen smiled, raised her hand so that her palm faced them, and the two Mayan women escorted them all out of the palace.

"Your Greatness," said Lupé when she was alone with her Queen.

"Yes, Lupé, my Chief Obtainer?"

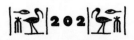

"The man and the bird and the camel … they were in the sacred cenote! They were soaking wet from its waters when they appeared before us. What if they drank from its sacredness before the waters had been diluted? What if the water entered their bodies?"

The Quetzal Queen smiled and stared through the grand archway. "They have been to the extremity, as the legends call it. Yet they do not know *where* they have been, or from what they have drunk. They are worthy, those three. Their lives can only enrich other things, and a little extra time will mean more enrichment. That can only make their world better. And besides, Lupé, sometimes knowledge can do more harm than good."

"Yes, my Queen."

"They will find out in time." The corners of the soft, youthful lips of the Quetzal Queen lifted in a wise smile. "And time shall stretch steadily before them, shall it not?"

"...AND, PERRY, THE LAST WE SAW of Bone, he was being carted off with his leg in the claws of that thing he got in Greece."

"Mmm?" muttered Gerald Perry Esquire as he, Jim, Doris, Brenda and Fifi sat in the clubroom of the Old Relics Society, back in Egypt. The late afternoon sunlight was drifting in through the tall windows and lighting up Fifi's blonde curls as she perched on the arm of Perry's big leather armchair in a convoluted lotus position. The sight of the sun in her hair had meant that Perry hadn't been paying much attention to what his friend had been telling him all afternoon.

"I said," Jim began again, "that the last—"

"Y'know, Jim," smiled Perry, his eyes twinkling like a young boy's, "I'm so immensely thrilled that you were able to get Fifi ... er, Mademoiselle Glusac ... back to me ... er, us. The world of theatre patrons, I mean."

"'Twas our pleasure," chirped Doris. "We don't mind a bit of an adventure, do we, Bren?"

Brenda moved her head in a wide circular motion as she sat cross-legged in the corner.

"Well, I want to stay put," announced Fifi, fluffing up her curls. "My travelling days are over for ze time being.

And ze first zing I shall do when I get 'ome is to get rid of zat feather collection of mine. It leads moi to nozzing but trouble!"

"Now look, Jim," Perry said in a slightly dreamy voice while he studied Fifi, "I really want to hear about how it all went and everything—"

"But, Perry, I've been telling you."

"—but not this afternoon. No, I tell you what we'll do. Why don't you all join me and Mademoiselle Glusac for a little celebration down in the Ephesus Effervescence Room? It's just down past the Society's library, take the fifth door after the Setiteti Bistro on the second floor, but watch out for Binkie Whiskin and his boring snail shells or you'll never—"

"Thank you, Perry." Jim smiled and stood. "But maybe some other time. I think we'd all like to get back to camp in the Valley of the Kings as soon as possible. Wouldn't we, gang?"

"Rark! Too right!" Doris was looking forward to Mrs Amun-Ra's special snail shergold cakes again.

"Quaaoo!" snorted Brenda, who had been thinking of her little patch of special sand and the unique worms she loved eating so much.

"I've been missing the sound of the wind as it moans in and out of all those tombs down there," Jim sighed wistfully.

Fifi unlocked her legs and stood. "Au revoir, Jim, Doris, Brenda. Zank you so much for all your 'elp."

"Yes, thank you, from the heart of my..." Perry

frowned. "No, from the bottom of my ... oh, you're a sight for old eyes, Fifi Glusac!" Perry gave Jim a big grin. "Thanks, my friend. I'll see you very soon, I'm sure. Now mind how you go, and if you see that Spong swinging from the light fixtures out there, give him a shout to come down. The lazy good-for-nothing!"

He took Fifi's arm and made his way out of the clubroom with her. "Now, come on, my dear, there's *lots* we have to talk about."

"Ooh la la," giggled Fifi as they disappeared into the corridor.

A different sort of man would have basked in the fame that could have come to him for making the sort of discovery that Cairo Jim had made at Uxmal in Mexico. A different sort of man would have told everyone about the existence of the Quetzal Queen and the "lost" Elixir of Eternity. A different sort of man would have got his photograph splashed across the newspapers worldwide, and would have cut the ribbons at the openings of bridges and roadways and fruit-juice factories, and would have attended many gala banquets in his own honour.

But not Jim of Cairo.

He did just as he had told Perry he would do: with Doris and Brenda he promptly and quietly slipped away to their camp in the Valley of the Kings.

One evening, soon after they had returned to camp, Doris flapped about and asked Jim why he hadn't

announced the discovery. He put down his pen (he was trying to write a poem at the time) and looked at her with a quizzical expression. "But why ever should I?" he asked.

"Because," spluttered the macaw, almost hopping off her perch in her exasperation, "you could have basked in the *glory* of it all. At least for a little time."

Cairo Jim smiled and tilted his pith helmet up until it cleared his forehead. "My dear," he said, reaching across and tousling her plumage, "I gave the Quetzal Queen my word. Besides, don't you think I have enough *glory* already? Look what I've got here ... the whispering sands of the Valleys, another breathtakingly tranquil evening under a star-studded sky, and the two dearest friends a human could wish for."

He looked across at Brenda, snout-deep in her new Melodious Tex book.

"Not to mention the exciting possibilities that lie buried beneath us. This," he whispered to Doris, "is *glory itself.*"

"Coo," cooed Doris, blinking it all in.

And the ever-aware Wonder Camel gave a snort of absolute agreement, for she knew – deep down in her humps – that the glory would last for a long, *long* time to come.

THE END

Swoggle me sideways!

Unearth more thrilling mysteries
of history starring Cairo Jim, Doris,
and Brenda the Wonder Camel –

THE CAIRO JIM
CHRONICLES

The Cairo Jim Chronicles,
read by Geoffrey McSkimming,
are available on CD
from Bolinda Audio Books!
See **www.bolinda.com** for details.